Ambigamist

Ambigamist

A NOVEL

LISA DALE

 publishing

Editing by Laurie Gibson
Cover and Layout Design by
    Golden Ratio Book Design
Published by Mu Publishing

For queries or information, contact:
lisa@mupeople.com

First Edition
ISBN: 978-1-7347896-0-7

For Giles
My One & Only

AUTHOR'S NOTE

The inspiration for *Ambigamist* came from my time working as a lawyer in Dubai from 2000 to 2016. Perhaps it's the result of studying Sociology alongside Law at University, but I found it intriguing to see the ways in which the laws of the United Arab Emirates differ from England – how in Dubai it's a crime to cohabit, to bounce a cheque, to have an abortion, to express a negative opinion about someone even if it's factual, but it's not a crime for a Muslim man to take multiple wives. In England, the opposite is true. Why?

Another theme of this novel is gender and its effect for women in the workplace. My own approach is to ignore it as a factor, to not let it be a self-imposed barrier to getting on, whether in the UK, the Middle East or elsewhere. For me, that helps, so I keep the gender of the protagonist in this story (Chris Jones) neutral. I invite you to decide whether, in your mind, Chris is male or female. Maybe have some fun alternating Chris' gender as you go along. I did when I was writing, and I found that Chris' achievements, mistakes, concerns and decisions would be the same, whether a man or a woman.

I know *Ambigamist* raises some tricky issues, but there's humour, too. After all, I'm retired from the law now, so I'm allowed to be less serious and more creative these days!

Finally, from the heaps of novels out there, thank you for choosing this one – I truly hope you enjoy the read.

Bigamy is having one wife too many. Monogamy is the same.
Oscar Wilde

Bigamy is having one husband too many. Monogamy is the same.
—Anonymous (a woman)
Erica Jong

PROLOGUE

The shriek of a child has me jumping to my feet and on the run. I'm across the deck and heading for the steps when the shriek repeats two, three times more. But wait, it hasn't come from below deck, has it? It's from overhead. I look up and catch the tail end of a gull, chasing hot on the heels of its mates, making a dash for home before night descends.

For god's sake Chris, get a grip! I tell myself as I go to sit back down. *The kids are fine, and so are you, and so is everyone else that matters from your messed up little world – everything has been taken care of. Just stick with the plan, that's all you need to do.*

But still, it's been three days on board this sodding boat and nobody's told me anything. The Somalis speak Arabic, but little of it, and I, being English, speak, well, only English. We're heading south, I know that from the North Star that's retreating further behind us with each passing night. There's land just in sight to our left, but it's not close enough to be swimmable and what land is it anyway? Portugal? Morocco? There are no lights twinkling, suggestive of human life, so it could be Western Sahara perhaps? I can't phone anyone, my mobile's long gone, thrown overboard on that first night, so I can only surmise what dire straits the rest of them are in. Crooked Amal will be banged up in some detention facility in Beirut, awaiting transfer to Dubai to face the music along with the equally crooked Lubna. Back in Pimlico, meanwhile, Alex will be high, drunk or both and taking comfort in the arms of lover boy James, futilely lamenting what's been lost. Abdullah's probably in London too, sent by Fatima on a fool's errand in search of missing family members, whilst Fatima will be keeping herself holed up in their Jumeirah mansion to avoid the neighbours and think about where it all went wrong. Al Shamsi will be up to his usual shenanigans on a fresh new deal, a fresh new Haddad by his side because the old Haddad will have been sent packing back to Lebanon, squarely framed to take the fall for any 'unfortunate repercussions' from last month's deal. But as for Tom, he'll be...

What the...?

A flicker of shadows and the sound of urgent whispers interrupt my inner ramblings. One of the kids appears on deck, followed quickly by the other. Spotting me, they shuffle their way over. The bigger of the two takes the little one by the hand and gives me a lopsided grin.

"We know we've asked you this before," he says, "but are we there yet?"

1.

Dubai
Four weeks earlier

We've been slogging it out for fifteen hours now and we're getting nowhere. The two guys sat across the table from us are blatant opportunists who seem to think they've sniffed out a fire sale. They're intent on grinding the deal of the century out of my client with their see-sawing antics and frankly I've had enough, but I owe it to Mark to hold out for his asking price.

"Forty million. That's our offer," says Marwan Al Shamsi. Unbelievable. We'd already shaken hands at fifty million dollars before agreeing to come into this boardroom yesterday afternoon and the only thing that has changed since then is my will to live brought on by a lost night's sleep. I have to hand it to him: the chairman of Shamal Enterprises is an indomitable old bugger. No wonder he's on the Forbes rich list.

The 'offer' is hanging in the air, waiting to be batted one way or the other. Mark shifts in his seat beside me and I hear him swallow. The early-morning call to prayer is filtering up from the mosque in the street below, intruding on the silence. Al Shamsi picks up his phone and starts tapping and scrolling, trying to appear indifferent to our reaction. The man sat next to him, introduced as his 'strategic investment adviser', is studying me intently over his half-rimmed glasses. Samer Haddad. We've met before – different place, different life – and his presence at the meeting is a niggling distraction.

I clear my throat to get Al Shamsi's attention. "You know that's well below the company's market value," I say, looking directly into his bloodshot eyes and willing myself not to blink. "We've sat here all night going through the finer details of the deal. What has come up to justify a twenty percent reduction in price? Did I miss something? If so, let's address it now. Otherwise, the price remains fifty million."

Al Shamsi raises his chin a notch and his hawkish nose twitches in disgust as if his gilded nostrils have been invaded by a sudden stench of sewer. "Time to pray," he says, pushing back his chair and getting to his feet. Haddad rises with him and the two of them troop out of the room, a crisp white kandoura followed by a grey pinstriped suit.

I take it as a positive sign that Al Shamsi and Haddad have chosen to take a break rather than bring our meeting to a close – it's a sure indication they're still in the game. "Just hang in there, Mark, we're nearly home and dry," I say, turning my attention to my client and giving his shoulder a squeeze. "We'll have this sewn up within the hour."

"I'm glad you think so, Chris. I honestly don't know what to think anymore except it has been a very long night and I'll be glad to get out of this god-awful boardroom." Mark looks as exhausted as he sounds as he rises stiffly out of his chair. He's not a well man nowadays – he's recently been diagnosed with chronic kidney disease – and the all-nighter has taken its toll. His face is grey with fatigue and I notice his hand trembling as he pours himself a glass of water. In that moment I see an old man, a frail imposter standing in my client's shoes. I'm slightly embarrassed for him and busy myself with wiping the remnants of sand off my own shoes. Most people would associate this stuff with a day at the seaside (buckets and spades, grit in the sandwiches, that sort of thing) but here in downtown Deira, the more, let's say, 'traditional' side of Dubai, you get sandy feet just from crossing the car park to reach your meeting.

I pull my laptop towards me and begin typing in final amendments to the Word document displayed on my screen. Our all-night discussions haven't resulted in many changes to the contract, but I'm dotting the i's and crossing the t's, determined to have an agreed form ready for the parties to sign before they leave this boardroom today.

"Okay, that's it." I hit *save* in a suitably resolute manner. "We're down to the price, and that's not changing." I flash Mark my most confident smile and grab a thumb drive out of my bag, ready to copy the document across for printing later.

"The last few years have been quite a roller-coaster ride, haven't they, Chris?" Mark's spirits have rallied during our short break and I find I can look him in the eye again. "I'm going to miss Dubai, that's for sure," he continues, "but it will be good to focus back on the London side of the business."

Talking of London, I should be on a flight back to Heathrow right now. In fact, by my reckoning, I should be fast asleep somewhere over Turkey. I'd texted Alex around two o'clock this morning: *Delayed in Dubai. Won't be home in time to take Josh to school. Sorry. Will call when I can x.* My phone has been buzzing in my pocket on a regular basis ever since. I suppose I'd better take a look before our buyers return for the final round.

Answer your damned phone are the words I catch on my screen as the boardroom door is thrown open and Al Shamsi and Haddad walk back in. Something's wrong at home, I know, but I can't leave the meeting now. I click off my phone and slip it back into my pocket. It will have to wait.

"Okay," says Al Shamsi, as soon as he's seated, "it's my daughter's birthday today so I'm in a generous mood." He pauses long enough for Mark and me to offer our *happy returns* to the absent birthday girl and then longer again to check he's got our full attention. "We'll close at fifty million," he says, "but first you must come through the due diligence clean. If we find any loose ends, we talk again. For now, let's get on with signing the papers and we can all get home in time for breakfast."

Al Shamsi and Mark are stretching across the boardroom table to shake hands whilst I'm grabbing the thumb drive and heading out the door, shouting for the office boy to help me with the printouts. I'm back within a few minutes, two contract copies in hand, which I place in front of Al Shamsi and Mark. I remind myself to breathe as I take my seat. "It's the same as the draft you reviewed last week, with a few amendments to take account of our discussions over the course of this meeting," I explain to them both. "All the amendments are summarised on the separate sheet at the back."

"Too long!" Al Shamsi's batting his hand at his copy contract as if he's shooing away a pesky fly. "Why do we need all these pages?" He tosses the document to Haddad, who picks it up with a sneer and weighs it in his fussy little hands like the prize twit he is.

"We're like brothers, Mark and me," Al Shamsi continues. "We don't need a complicated contract, just to keep in the drawer and never read again." He turns his attention to my client. "You trust me, no?"

This isn't the first time I've been made out to be the bad guy by doing my job, setting down in black and white what's going to happen when the rosy relationship between the parties loses its bloom, and I've got a response at the ready. "You're absolutely right, Mr Al Shamsi," I say. "My client trusts you as, of course, you do him. But the contract's there for the benefit of everyone else. You've negotiated a very complex deal here, and we need a document that explains it all." Al Shamsi sits up a notch and flexes his shoulders as I continue. "Your executive team will want to see the detail, not to mention your auditors, bankers..."

Throughout this exchange, Haddad has been busily flicking through the contract, tutting and frowning as he scans the pages. Now he sets the document down squarely in front of him, sits back and folds his arms.

"Hmmph."

"Well? What's the verdict?" Al Shamsi demands. He won't sign a thing without the green light from Haddad but, even so, the irritable edge in his voice contains a warning: *don't go overcomplicating this.*

Haddad peers at me over his glasses and smirks as we lock eyes. I wish he'd stop looking at me like he knows something I don't – it's putting me on edge.

"We can live with it."

Prize twit or not, I feel like hugging him when I hear those glorious words.

Ten minutes later the contract has been signed with a closing date fixed for four weeks from today subject, of course, to a clean due diligence report. Al Shamsi and Mark are back-slapping and hand-shaking like the brothers they're supposed to be. *Mabrook! Congratulations!* Meanwhile, I'm gathering up my papers so I can exit the boardroom as quickly as decorum allows. I need to get in touch with home and see what's going on.

When Haddad comes up to me and pulls me roughly towards him, I think it's to drag me into the celebrations, or maybe to thank me for handling the legals, but instead he grabs my arm and spits words into my ear that reverberate right down my spine. "You think you're so clever, but I know what you are." He's squeezing my arm tight and I turn away to avoid inhaling his stagnant breath. "I've got you now," he sneers, releasing me from his grip and walking away. This guy isn't mucking about and the raw truth of my situation is sinking in fast.

Four weeks to closing, that's all I've got. It's not nearly long enough to unravel this mess that is my life.

2.

Dubai
Twenty-Eight days to Closing

Alex isn't picking up the bloody phone, but it's only five o'clock in the morning back in London – they're three hours behind Dubai – so that's okay, isn't it? Alex and Josh will both be tucked up in their beds fast asleep, oblivious to the Thursday-morning clunking and clanging of the binmen that would have me up and about by now if I were there. Whatever the problem was during the night, it can't have been too serious.

On a good day you'd make this journey in twenty minutes, but today isn't going to be one of those days. We've come to a standstill on the highway leading to the airport and haven't moved an inch for aeons. Drivers are honking their horns up and down the five lines of stationary traffic with the sole purpose, it seems, of offloading their stress on to the rest of us. Mark's personal assistant has got me booked on the nine-forty to Heathrow, but at this rate I'm not going to make the flight – it's already eight o'clock and the growing wail of sirens behind us isn't a good sign.

"Pileup on the Airport Road off-ramp," reports Mark's driver, who's straining his head out the window to get a better look up ahead. "A minibus and five or six cars minimum," he adds, pulling his head back in within a hair's breadth of getting it knocked off by a motorbike whizzing past.

"Is it totally blocked up there, or is some traffic still getting through?" I ask, but Mohan just looks at me in the rear-view mirror and wobbles his head. *Yes? No? Maybe?* Could be any of them really. I'll take it as a *maybe*. The sirens are getting louder so I check out the back window and see a police car and ambulance a hundred metres or so back, lights flashing, followed closely by a tow truck, all slowly cutting through the traffic to reach the pileup. Fingers crossed we'll be on the move again soon, for my sake as well as for Mark's. It was good of him to offer to drop me at the airport after the meeting and I'm feeling bad for getting him snarled up in all this traffic. He could have been home in bed by now, catching up on his lost night's sleep. I'm about to thank him when my phone vibrates in my jacket pocket. It's Alex calling. I mouth an apology instead and connect the call.

"We're in casualty at St Thomas' Hospital." Alex's tone is strained, accusing almost. "Josh fell down the stairs last night."

"Oh Christ! Is he okay?" I feel an instant rush of adrenaline flood through my body, pushing away the fog of fatigue. "What happened?"

"He cut his head open and needed stitches, but he's also been sick a few times and he's complaining of a sore neck, so they did a CT scan a couple of hours ago and put him in a cervical collar. The nurses won't tell me anything – they just say I have to wait for the doctor to come and speak to me." Alex's voice is shaking. "Chris, I'm really worried."

"Okay, look, I'm going to get there as soon as I can, alright? A few hours, that's all." It's gone quiet at the other end of the line and for a moment I think our connection's been lost, but then I make out the sound of Alex's sniffles. "Anyway," I continue, "I'm sure he's going to be fine. Remember that time he decided he was Buzz Lightyear and let go of the swing? He was convinced he could fly and ended up smacking face-first into the ground. Grazes, that's all he got. Kids bounce."

I'm not believing my bullshit, by the way, I'm actually freaking out, but Alex needs the reassurance and I'm not there to give it, am I?

We end the call with Alex promising to keep me updated about Josh's condition, and me promising to keep Alex updated on the progress of my journey home.

"I heard all of that," says Mark, as I disconnect. "Is the little guy okay?"

"I hope so. Thanks. And sorry for dragging you through all of this." The broad sweep of my arm is aimed at the crappy traffic as well as my latest domestic emergency. Mark doesn't need any of this extra hassle.

"The traffic's moving again," reports Mohan, putting the car into gear and inching us slowly forwards. "They've cleared a lane up there. It's just rubberneckers slowing us down now," he complains, sticking his head out the window for a good gawp anyway. But as soon as we get past the wreckage, his foot's down on the accelerator and we're away.

I plonk my passport on the check-in counter at eight thirty-five. "I'll use my miles to upgrade to first, if I may," I tell the guy behind the desk. Once I get on board I need a shower, then I need to work, and then I need to sleep. Besides, my

Emirates miles won't be any use to me after next month so I'd just as well use them now. I'm handed a boarding pass for seat number 2A and told to go straight to the gate.

I'm a list maker. I have a list for everything, including a master list of all my other lists. I know it's bad, but it's how I keep control of my double troubled life. An hour into the flight and I've already typed up my 'Bailey's Dubai Closing Check-list', sub-divided into 'Things to do – Legal' (in other words, me) and 'Things to do – Admin & Finance' and now I've moved on to the 'Due Diligence Requirements' list. This consists of all the documents we need to produce to Shamal Enterprises ahead of closing next month, with a note next to each item indicating where it's filed or who to contact to get hold of it. When I've finished, I email it all to Dimple, my secretary over at Bailey's Dubai. She can send Admin and Finance their list and make a start on the due diligence stuff herself whilst I'm in London over the next few days. She'll be at her desk by now, so I decide to give her a call.

She picks up on the first ring. "Good morning, Chris. Dimple with you this side." The line's a bit crackly, but it's amazing there's any connection at all when I'm calling from a plane thirty thousand feet above the earth's surface. "I've received your email," I can just make out her saying. "Don't worry, Chris. You can leave it all with me."

Don't go thinking Dimple's always this model of efficiency – she can be really scatty at times, infuriating actually, but I can rely on her to give one hundred percent to the job, plus she's got my back. I'm going to bloody miss her when I've gone.

Next up, I need to find out about Josh's CT scan results. I call Alex's number and feel my stomach lurch when I hear

a faint "hello" at the other end of the line. Is that relief or
anguish I can detect?

"What's the news, Alex?" I say.

"The doctor says he's got a br…"

And then the line goes dead.

3.

London

I must have tried Alex's number a hundred times over the last eight hours with the same result over and over again – sodding voicemail – so by the time I reach St Thomas' I'm in total panic mode. I've managed to narrow Josh's condition down to two possibilities, brain haemorrhage or broken neck. What else could it be?

The cab drops me off outside A&E and I head inside. Now 'Joanne Price Trainee Receptionist' is making a meal of finding Josh's name on the computer. "Josh Jones, you say...erm...nope, he's not in Emergency...erm...just bear with me a sec." She picks up the phone and makes a call, taps on her keyboard some more, watches the screen, waits. This is excruciating. "Okay, found him. Oh yes, I remember now," she says, frowning at the screen. "The little blond lad. He's been moved to the Acute Admissions Ward. Follow the blue arrows. Down the corridor, left at the..." But I'm already off, rushing along the corridor in the direction of the blue arrows as quickly as my knackered legs can carry me.

A nurse directs me to Josh's room and I find him alone and sleeping when I get there. His head's all bandaged up, but he looks comfortable enough. There aren't any tubes or wires coming out of him, no cervical collar around his neck, no machines bleeping anywhere. I take Josh's hand and give it a squeeze to see if I can get a reaction.

"You made it!" Alex comes breezing into the room, carrying a steaming Styrofoam cup in one hand and an *Evening Standard* newspaper in the other.

"The dreaded reviews are out," Alex says, waving the newspaper around.

"Bugger the reviews, Alex, you're not even in the show! What's going on with Josh?"

"I've told you."

"No, you haven't told me anything, Alex, because your phone's flat – again – and you haven't bothered to find a pay phone to call me."

"But I didn't know your number – it's stored on my phone."

Urrrgh!

"Anyway, I told you when we last spoke. Josh is fine. They're just keeping him in for a few hours under observation and then we can take him home."

"But you were telling me they'd found something. Remember? When we last spoke? You said he had something beginning with 'br'."

Alex is looking at me like I'm demented, but then the penny seems to drop.

"Oh, I'm so sorry, Chris. No, I was making a joke. I was saying they'd found a *brain*: despite all our doubts, he's got a *brain* in his head."

You have got to be bloody kidding me.

Put it down to relief, exhaustion maybe, the stress of the last twenty-four hours, anxiety for the future, lack of something proper to eat, all of the above most probably, but my legs will no longer hold me up. I collapse into the visitors chair and, I'm sorry to say, I start to cry.

"Everything okay in here?" The doctor comes sweeping into the room, firing her question in my direction – whether *to* me or *about* me, I don't know – and grabs the clinical notes hooked over the end of Josh's bed. Then she's up at the head of the bed, inspecting Josh's dressings, feeling his cheek with the back of her hand. "Good. Yes, very good. You can take him home when he wakes up. The nurse will talk you through how to care for the head wound, but there's nothing serious for you to worry about."

Then she's gone, off to finish her rounds, and we've got the green light to coax our son awake. I take his hand and give it a gentle squeeze, and bend to kiss his cheek. His hand feels warm and clammy but his cheek is cooler. "Hey Josh, time to wake up, buddy," I say into his ear, but he just scrunches up his face and rolls the other way. When we've eventually got him sat up and chatting, albeit a bit groggily, I bring the conversation round to the events of the night before – what was he doing up at that time of night and what caused him to fall down the stairs?

His account of what happened is chilling.

"Margo was barking so I got up to see what was wrong with her," he explains. "I saw a man in the hallway downstairs kicking at Margo, so I ran to save her and tripped and fell down the stairs."

So whilst I was in Dubai haggling over the non-consequential details of a business deal, some scumbag was breaking into my house back home with my family fast asleep upstairs. *Angry indignation*, that's how novelists would describe it, but it isn't nearly enough to cover what

I'm feeling right now. Thank God I got Margo last year – this could all have been a whole lot worse if the intruder hadn't been frightened off.

"You called the police, right?" I say, glancing at Alex.

"No need," says Alex, with a shrug of the shoulders. "There was nobody there when *I* got downstairs. The doctor says Josh is just confused from the knock on his head."

"That's not true, Mum! That man was real," says Josh, exasperated. "He was wearing a long coat and a hat with a brim, just like in the gangster movies. He ran away when he saw me, and he won't be coming back, that's for sure, with Margo and me guarding the house."

My son is giving me that beseeching look he sometimes has when it comes to Alex: *I know I'm the nine-year-old here, but you've got to believe me.* In any event, he sounds pretty clear-headed to me, despite the head injury. He's not usually one for making things up, either. That's Alex's domain.

"If you hadn't bought him that bloody dog, waking us up with her barking all night, none of this would have happened," snaps Alex. *Terrific!* Alex is the one who's supposed to be taking care of things back home whilst I'm away earning a living. That's the deal. How did all this become my fault?

Whatever, I'm sickened my son has gone through this.

Josh and Alex are both looking at me now, as if I'm somehow going to supply all the answers and make it all right again. My phone starts to vibrate in my pocket, badgering to be answered, but I'm too preoccupied to do anything about it: *Long coat. Brimmed hat. Gangster. Crap.* I've worked out the identity of our midnight intruder and it isn't good.

"Come on," I say, "let's just get home."

4.

I'd rather be working from home today to keep an eye on Josh, but I've got a meeting with my managing partner at eleven o'clock that I can't miss. At least Alex is there, for what it's worth: judging from the empties under the sink this morning, the *'dreadful trauma'* of *'dealing single-handedly, darling'* with Josh's *'absolutely horrifying'* hospital ordeal needed to be washed away with more than one bottle of Chianti long after I'd gone to bed last night. I sound bitter, I know, but even by Alex's standards it was a lot of booze and I suspect the resulting hangover will get more nursing today than our poor lad.

Perhaps I can get away early, once I've finished my meeting. For the past few weeks the firm's partners have been looking at opening a branch office of Coulter & Co in Dubai, something I'm very keen to see happen for personal reasons, and today I'm hoping to get the green light on the project.

It was back in 2012 that I'd first got involved with the city when I picked up the phone to Mark Bailey one day.

"Know anything about Dubai, Chris?" he'd asked.

At the time, I had no idea what strife this seemingly innocuous question would get me into. Would I still have picked up the phone so readily, had I known? That's a tough one. Anyway, I'd been Mark's go-to lawyer in London for about five years by then and I knew vaguely he'd had some involvement in real estate development in Dubai, but after the global financial crisis in 2008 and 2009 it hadn't come up in any of our discussions. I just assumed he'd walked away from it.

"Trust Dubai to have the balls to bounce back!" he'd continued during that fateful call. "Now I'm going to have to sort myself out over there and I need your help."

"I'm listening, go on," I'd said, my interest piqued. This was a place I'd wanted to visit and see for myself for some time.

"Did I ever mention the Jumanah Heights master community project to you?" he'd continued. "I bought a plot of land there back in 2007 and was getting ready to launch a twenty-eight storey apartment building. The idea was to sell the apartment units off-plan and use the sale proceeds to fund the construction. All the developers were doing it, and the investors were queuing around the clock to snap the units up. Dubai had recently relaxed its laws to allow real estate in designated areas of the city to be bought by foreigners and projects couldn't be launched fast enough. It was like a feeding frenzy – real boom time. And then Lehman Brothers collapsed and we all held our breath to see what ripple effect this would have on the city."

As Mark continued to lay out his situation, I'd quickly searched 'Dubai global financial crisis 2008' on my desktop and scrolled through the results:

September 18 **2008**: **Dubai** dispels investors' concerns following the fall of Lehman Brothers. Declares itself to be 'recession proof'.

October 04 **2008**: **Dubai** property prices jumped 78% between Q1 of 2007 and Q1 of **2008**. Recent price correction is 'welcomed' by real estate professionals.

November 17 **2008**: American professionals head for **Dubai** to ride out the **financial crisis**.

"A stupendous credit crunch – that was the effect," Mark had continued. "Banks stopped lending to investors, who stopped funding developers, who couldn't pay the construction companies, who downed tools and stopped work. Twenty percent of the world's cranes were deployed on Dubai's construction sites back in 2008 and by late 2009 every one of them had come to an abrupt standstill. The off-plan sector was toxic and the property market had crashed in spectacular fashion."

Indeed, headlines from that time, I saw, painted a doomsday scenario:

January 14 2009: From soaring ambitions to desert sand, **Dubai**'s hedonistic dream is over – **Dubai** has suffered the world's steepest property slump in the **global** recession. Property prices drop 50 percent from their **2008** peak.

July 04 2009: **Dubai**'s airport 'clogged with cars' abandoned by expat workers fleeing from threat of prison for unpaid debts.

September 25 2009: Recession hits glitzy **Dubai** as the bubble bursts. Markets fear the gulf emirate will struggle to pay its debt as cash runs dry.

"So I mothballed my project and I'd pretty much written it off," Mark had continued. "Then, right out of the blue today, I get an email from Zakheen, the master developer of Jumanah Heights. Sniffing a recovery in the market, they've re-booted the master community infrastructure works and now they're asking me and all the other plot developers for our next instalment payments."

The more current search results I'd seen on my screen did indeed support the notion of a miraculous-style recovery in the city's real estate sector:

March 04 2012: What real estate crash? Boom times are back for **Dubai** as property prices top pre-recession highs.

April 15 2012: **Dubai**'s towering ambitions return as the economy begins to prosper once more.

June 20 2012: From **crisis** to recovery: vital reforms have been put in place to stabilise the economy as debt falls 74% since **2008**.

In short, with no proceeds from off-plan unit sales in the coffers and no prospect of borrowing the money from nervous banks, back in 2012 Mark was facing the prospect of losing his plot as well as all the cash he'd already injected into the project.

This is the dilemma I took to Tom Fletcher back then. He was a South African expat lawyer working in Dubai for the local firm Al Hattan & Co and he had a good reputation for his real estate work. Well, Tom was brilliant. Within a few days, he'd orchestrated a settlement with Zakheen that saw Mark down-size to a much smaller plot where he could build a modest five-storey apartment block, still within the prestigious Jumanah Heights estate. The money Zakheen had already received from Mark for the larger plot was sufficient not only to pay for the smaller plot outright, but it also gave Mark 'change' in the form of credit notes he could sell on the open market for cash to kick-start the construction on the smaller site. When the building was completed in early 2013, the property market was still weak so Mark repackaged the building as 'branded serviced residences' and entered the short-term corporate rentals market. This proved very lucrative and over the years Mark repeated the formula in various of the city's new 'freehold for foreigners' designated areas until he'd built up a substantial portfolio of properties netting millions in rent annually. This is the company we're selling to Marwan Al Shamsi in four weeks' time, once we clear the due diligence.

Anyway, back in 2012 Mark had been so confident with the outcome of the Zakheen negotiations that he'd opened an office in Dubai and seconded me to work there three days a week – a lucrative arrangement that both Coulter & Co and I had readily agreed to.

And now here I am, seven years later, facing the prospect of this cushy arrangement coming to an end the moment Mark's sale of Bailey's Dubai closes next month. Unless I can find another role where I can continue working between

Dubai and London, I'm headed full throttle into the buffers with everyone still aboard. I'm banking on a new Coulter's office there to provide the solution. I'd first planted the seed of the idea in John Coulter's ear two months back when Mark first announced his intentions to sell up in Dubai and had put me on notice my role there would be coming to an end. John was keen to explore the idea, telling me that the firm's Executive Committee was in bullish mood for international expansion and that a presence in the Middle East would be a good strategic fit, so I'd gone ahead and prepared the feasibility report.

My presentation of the report to the Executive Committee last week had gone well enough, but had I sufficiently dazzled the attending lineup of jaded senior partners to see a Coulter's office in Dubai go from vision to reality? It's hard to say.

"*Connecting Minds, Creating the Future* – the theme for the World Expo 2020 being hosted by Dubai next year," I'd told them. "And the city is a living and breathing embodiment of that theme. Robotics, artificial intelligence, renewables, smart city initiatives, the Internet of Things, blockchain, the Fourth Industrial Revolution, 3D printing – it's all happening there. They're aspiring to be the happiest city on the planet by being at the forefront of embracing smart technology."

"Happiest city?" piped up one of the partners. "The last time I went to Dubai, I couldn't even access their public Wi-Fi with my UK phone and when I tried to Skype the office from there it was blocked by the authorities. Didn't make me very happy, I can tell you."

This was Malcolm Thomas, who everyone knows is the grumpy one, especially nowadays after his wife left him for a London Underground tube driver she met on a writing retreat in Yorkshire last year, so I'd decided to put his grumblings aside and plough on through.

"The point is," I'd said, "these government-led initiatives will be the springboard for Dubai's next spectacular growth spurt, attracting a new wave of multinational corporations to come and set up there as well as bringing billions of dollars of foreign direct investment into the city.

"I propose we focus on presenting Coulters as the pre-eminent law firm for green energy and technology, focusing on our experience here in the UK working for clients in the renewables sector and marketing that in Dubai. We'll write articles for all the right publications, get our lawyers speaking on all the right conference panels, offer pro-bono legal work to all the right government departments – that apparently works very well out there – and we'll collaborate with selected top-tier local firms and bid jointly for the work, offering our specialist industry knowledge in conjunction with their local know-how. It's a winning formula. And once we get closer to the local firms we can market our UK credentials to their clients and start sending work back here to the London office.

"And of course, Dubai is a hub for the whole Middle East region. Once we're set up, we can look further afield for work – Saudi, Bahrain, Kuwait and so on. Not to mention Abu Dhabi, right on the doorstep. I've drawn up a list of our existing clients who already have some form of business presence in the Middle East. We can tap into those first.

"I propose we start with two permanent lawyers on the ground there, selected from our Energy and Technology practices, and I would be pleased to put myself forwards as the managing partner of the office, bridging the gap between Dubai and our head office here in London. As you know, I've been commuting backwards and forwards for several years already in my secondment role with Mark Bailey's company, so it would be no problem for me to keep a similar travel routine going."

I had then taken them through all the setup costs, the financial projections for the first five years of operations, licensing requirements for our office and lawyers there, Emiratisation quotas for hiring staff, and so on.

"We'd have to keep a tight leash on the junior partners," had been the only comment at the end of my presentation, this coming from Jonathon Knox, the head of our Banking and Finance practice. "They'll be spending their whole marketing budget on business development trips to Dubai if we let them. Rugby Sevens, tennis championships, horse races, golfing tournaments, not to mention the Formula One down in Abu Dhabi." Besides that minor caveat, they'd all seemed relatively enthused with the prospect of seeing a Coulters in Dubai, so I'm quietly hopeful.

My office phone rings and I'm summoned to John Coulter's office up on the top floor.

"So, Chris," John begins as soon as I'm settled. "The Executive Committee has reached a decision and I'm afraid it's not what you want to hear."

Oh shit!

"With our plans for expansion into Hong Kong and New York already underway, and with the global economic weakness, now's just not the right time for us to venture into Dubai as well."

No, no, no, this can't be happening...

"We can look at it again towards the end of next year, see how things are going then."

That will be much too late!

"But for now, we look forward to having you back full-time in the London office once the sale of Mark's company over there closes."

This is a complete disaster.

"Don't worry, we've plenty of clients here in London who can use your Middle East experience. There'll be no problem keeping you busy. I expect you'll be pleased to be back home permanently at long last."

That's just it. *Home.* They say home is where the heart is. How can I be pleased when half my heart is back in Dubai?

Now what am I going to do?

5.

London
Twenty-Four days to Closing

"Good work last week, Chris. Fifty million dollars, right on the nose."

Mark and I have met up for after-work drinks at a casino in Mayfair. It's not one of our usual haunts, but he's got it into his head the development of Vegas-style super casinos in the UK is his next big business opportunity, so here we are sat up at the bar, 'getting a better feel for the industry'. We're still weeks away from completing the sale of Bailey's Dubai, but it seems the proceeds are already as good as spent.

"Those Shamal guys really know how to haggle, but you got us over the line," Mark says. "My only slight regret is my name's being sold along with the company. *Bailey.* I know it's got brand value attached to it, but it's also personal, you know? I just hope Al Shamsi doesn't do anything to tarnish it. Anyway, here's to a smooth closing," he says, clinking his glass of Perrier against mine. (We'd both prefer something stronger, obviously, but Mark's doctor's instructions to lay off the booze are being strictly monitored by his wife,

Grace, and my excuse is my head's throbbing and I'm trying to avoid a full-on migraine.)

"The company's worth every cent, and they know it," I tell him. "It was just a matter of holding the line with them."

"Quite honestly, I'd rather have walked away from the deal than come down on the agreed price. It's a matter of principle – I didn't sweat blood out there in the sandpit to let it all go for less than it's worth."

Mark's got a point. It's not really the best time to be selling up in Dubai, with the markets weak. He's only doing it because he's sick and needs to ease off on the workload for a while. *Speaking of which, I wonder if Grace knows about his grand plans to open the next Caesar's Palace somewhere in the Home Counties? I must touch base with her before my next trip to Dubai.*

"Let's hope we clear their due diligence okay. Are we expecting any snags with that, Chris?"

"No, not at all," I assure Mark. "We've got eighty percent of the documents together already. We just need to get the rest from the old files in store and then upload everything to the data room. I'm working with Dimple on it and we'll have it all done by early next week."

"Great, I don't want to give Al Shamsi any excuses to re-open the deal. It'll be good to get this over and done with next month."

I wish I could share Mark's sentiment, but I've got plenty of reasons to see the sale drag out. I need to keep my UK/UAE gig going for as long as possible – another fifteen years would be about right – so I've got a rather unusual conflict of interest with my client. Am I tempted to scupper Mark's deal to keep hold of my secondment role in his company? *Don't even think about it; there will be another solution.*

It's at this moment Mark's phone starts vibrating, buzzing against the glass bar top like an angry wasp and clawing us back from our diverging thoughts. "I'd better take this," Mark says, picking up. "It's Geoff calling from Dubai. It's gone eleven over there – something must be up."

Geoff is Mark's brother-in-law, the owner of a lucrative vintage car dealership in the UK with designs on replicating his success out in the Gulf. Tom's been helping him out this week with the various legal arrangements involved with opening his showrooms – in Dubai, Abu Dhabi and Riyadh 'to begin with'.

"Have you got Tom's personal mobile number by any chance?" Mark swivels on his stool to direct the question at me. "Geoff's got himself into some sort of trouble with the police and they're holding him in Bur Dubai police station. He's trying to get hold of Tom to see if he can help, but his work phone's on voicemail."

I pull up Tom's number and hand my phone across to Mark. Listening in to Mark's end of the conversation, I'm trying to piece together what the problem is: "...That's right, zero tolerance...There must be a logical explanation... You were out with Saudis, you say?...mmm, mmm...I understand...We'll try to get hold of Tom as well... Look, don't worry, we'll make sure someone gets down there to help you as soon as possible."

"I don't bloody believe it!" Mark says, disconnecting the call. "Geoff's been picked up for drink driving, but he swears he hasn't had a single drop of alcohol all night!"

The typical outcome for these kinds of offences in Dubai is a month behind bars, often followed by deportation. This is serious stuff. I call Tom and his line's engaged. I'm hoping he's on the phone to Geoff. I keep trying and manage to get through on my fifth redial.

"You spoke to Geoff?" I say, dispensing with any preamble.

"I'm on my way to the police station now." Tom's reply is easy, reassuring. "Sounds like there's been some sort of mix-up, from what Geoff has told me so far," he continues, "but don't worry, you can leave it with me."

Those are the words I need to hear. "Thanks, Tom, you're a real star," I tell him, and hang up.

I'm feeling rather proud of Tom, actually, for stepping up to the plate in the hour of need: it would have been easy for him to fob the problem off onto one of the junior litigation lawyers in his firm – after all, they're all local Emiratis and speak the lingo – but he's chosen to handle the situation himself.

"Tom's very good, isn't he?" Mark says, echoing my thoughts. "How's he getting on at Al Hattan & Co?"

"Great! He loves it there. He's hoping to be made a partner soon, the first expat in his firm to manage it."

"He won't be looking to leave Dubai any time soon, then?"

"No chance."

"On the other hand, Chris, I get the feeling you're sorry to be leaving Dubai?"

"Yes, I suppose I am." I shrug and take a sip of water. "If you spend half your time in a place, you're going to get attached."

I don't know why, but Mark's studying me closely.

"There's something more to it than that, though," he says. "It's Tom, isn't it?"

Whoa, stop right there! How the hell did Mark get that idea into his head?

"What do you mean? What's Tom?"

"Why you're reluctant to pack things up there – you don't want to leave Tom."

I haven't told Mark about my personal situation, so I've no idea where this has come from, but in any event he's got it all wrong and I tell him so.

"Then if you like Dubai so much, why don't you find yourself a full-time job out there and move Alex and Josh over to be with you?"

Urrrgh! This is not helping. My migraine's really threatening to make itself known now and I squint to ease the tension. Mark gives my shoulder a squeeze, sensing, I think, that his suggestions are wide of the mark. He excuses himself to visit the washroom and I ask the barman for another sparkling water: I need to take a paracetamol before this pain gets any worse. I reach for my bag and my phone buzzes so I grab my phone instead, half expecting it to be Tom. But no, it's a text message from that slimeball, Samer Haddad:

I believe you have a personal dilemma we can usefully discuss. Call me.

I drop my phone on the bar and gulp down the paracetamol with an eye-watering swig of Perrier.

6.

Dubai
Twenty-One days to Closing

I could do with Dimple being on form today, but she's in one of her scatty moods. She'd like to blame it on me, piling her up with too many chores, but she was already in a tizzy before she'd even stepped outside her apartment this morning. How do I know this, you may ask. Was I there? No. Is there something amiss about her appearance that's giving the game away? Not really – her salwar kameez is all present and correct in its shocking pinkness and accessorized with the usual glittering profusion of jangling gold jewellery. So, how do I know? Well, from a simple request for her brother's mobile number. "It's saved on my phone," she'd said, rummaging around in her handbag and retrieving what looked like a remote control for a television. "Oh," she'd then said, "I think I've left my phone at home on the settee." Undeterred, she then called her mobile number from the office landline and her son picked up. After giving the poor lad an earwigging (he was supposed to be at his auntie's helping to paint the kitchen, not sat time-wasting on the settee all day) she finally got Rajeev's number off him and handed it to me on a Post-it note. She was looking far more pleased with herself than the circumstances merited if you ask me, but at least I've got her brother's number now. He's one of the senior instructors up at the flight school in Fujairah and I want to ask if they'd be interested in taking my Cessna off me. I'll give him a call later when I'm at the airport.

Between us, Dimple and I have managed to track down most of the due diligence documents for the Shamal deal and we spent this morning uploading them to the virtual data room. We're stuck now until the old files arrive from storage and we can start trawling through them to find the remaining documents. Dimple's been on the phone to various people at the storage company throughout the afternoon, trying to get the files delivered to us urgently. Regardless, I'm due back to London tonight so we won't be able to finish the job until I return later in the week. That's okay, though: there's still three weeks until closing.

I've only got a couple of hours before I need to depart for the airport, so I decide to leave Dimple to it and go home to freshen up. I'm feeling knackered, thanks to Tom. He kept me out late last night, helping him to enjoy the best of Dubai's six-star hospitality courtesy of a very grateful Geoff Townsend. It isn't my usual type of hang-out to be honest, it's too fussy, but I'm learning to keep an open mind, plus I hadn't heard the details of Geoff's miraculous jailbreak yet and I was keen to get the full story.

"So come on, out with it. How'd you manage it?" I'd asked as soon as the sommelier had filled our glasses and left us to it.

"Well, let's see," he'd said, sipping his champagne. "Oh, now that's good."

"Tom, come on!"

"Okay, okay. So when I got down to the police station, Geoff was still adamant he hadn't drunk any alcohol all night. He'd been having dinner at the Fairmont, entertaining a couple of car importers from Saudi. They're not drinking, so he's not drinking. Anyway, Dubai has a zero-tolerance policy for drink-driving, right? Why take the risk when it's easy enough to get a taxi back to your hotel at the end of the night?"

"True, go on."

"So, how does a guy who's been drinking watermelon coolers all evening end up with alcohol in his system?"

White wine sauce? Brandy in the tiramisu? I still couldn't see where Tom was going with this.

"And how come, out of all the cars on the Sheikh Zayed Road that night, it was Geoff's hire car that got pulled over? It didn't add up to me, so I decided to go over to the Fairmont and see if I could persuade security to show me the footage from the restaurant surveillance cameras. I had a hunch from hearing similar stories before."

The waiter had presented us both with some sort of appetizer at this point, going by the fancy name *amuse-bouche*. It looked like a laboratory specimen in a petri dish to me, and it smelt like the unwashed bilges of a fishing trawler. "A set-up, you mean?" I'd said, pushing the plate away.

"Exactly. The camera footage showed two men lurking around the barman whilst he was preparing drinks for Geoff's table. The barman turned his back for a moment and one of the men sloshed a generous measure of clear liquid into each of the three glasses. He had one of those liquor bottles shaped like a hip flask stashed in his pocket. D'you know the ones I mean? Anyway, Geoff and his dinner guests agreed the mocktails were pretty good, except they weren't mocktails, were they? They'd been laced with gin. The two goons stayed sat at the bar, waiting for Geoff's party to leave, then one of them called the police, tipping them off to a drunk guy getting behind the wheel of a car at the Fairmont hotel. Turns out the two goons were hired by a local vintage car dealer intent on seeing Geoff out of business before he'd even got started. The three of them are behind bars now, facing prosecution."

I'm miles away, recounting this story in my head, when the taxi draws up outside my villa. This has been my home in Dubai for the last seven years, now shared with two other people in my life. I walk up the path, unlock the front door and let myself in.

"I'm home," I shout and I hear squealing and a quick pitter-patter of little feet across tiles. An exuberant toddler comes running down the corridor, arms flung wide ready to be hoisted off her feet and swept up into a tight hug. This is my beautiful daughter, Noura. My maid makes an appearance at the kitchen door. Amal must be out. I gaze down at Noura and notice I'm wearing the wrong wedding ring. I slip it off, dropping it into my bag.

So now you know: I am a bigamist.

7.

London
Twenty days to Closing

"Did you remember the Bollinger, darling?"

In Alex's mind, my trips to Dubai have somehow become synonymous with duty-free shopping opportunities. You have to wonder whether I'd be allowed back across my Pimlico threshold if I weren't laden down with bags of clinking bottles. It's got so bad Mark calls me Alex's booze mule. "Bloody cart-horse, more like," I mumble as I haul my wheelie bag, brief case and obligatory clinking bottles over the doorstep.

"What was that, darling?" says Alex, emerging from the kitchen.

"I said, you'll need to put it all in the freezer if you want to serve it cold this evening."

"Ooooh, lovely!" says Alex, inspecting the contents of the duty-free bags and whisking them away. "I'm soooo excited – all the guys from the show have confirmed and it's all going to be such wonderful fun."

Absolutely. Happy for you. Sounds terrific.

I have to tolerate these friends of Alex; it's an unspoken part of the bargain we'd reached nine years ago when Josh had come along unplanned and Alex, a struggling actor, had reluctantly taken on the role of the stay-at-home parent whilst I carried on in my legal career and became the main breadwinner. There's resentment there, bubbling beneath the surface, and putting up with a thespian evening here and there serves as a welcome release for Alex and a kind of penance for me.

As I'm bouncing my wheelie bag up the stairs, Alex is chirping instructions from the kitchen: "Be a sweetie and come help me set up as soon as you're showered. The traffic home from Josh's karate class was horrendous and I'm hideously behind in here, darling. The salad needs washing, the veggies need chopping…"

Bloody marvellous! Never mind I've been travelling all night and working all day – we're in Alex's world now, so none of that is given a second thought. I pop my head round Josh's door and find him sprawled on his bed with Margo, still wearing his karate outfit. The bandage on his head is gone, I see, replaced with a pink Band-Aid covering the gash on his left temple. He shouldn't have gone to karate this week whilst he still had stitches, but I wasn't here to make the decision, was I?

"How's it going, buddy?" I go over to give my son a kiss. "I've missed you." Josh is used to my to-ing and fro-ing and takes it in his stride, after all he was barely out of nappies when I first started going to Dubai. It helps that I try to make him feel included in that part of my life, to paint him a picture about what it's like there (whilst skirting around the bits about my other family, obviously).

"Did anything exciting happen this time?" he asks. "Any good stories to tell me?"

"Well, let me think," I say, scratching my head. *Did I tell you the one about your little sister and how she tried to... Okay, maybe not.* "My friend Tom told me a good one the other day," I offer.

"Tom. That's the other lawyer you know there, isn't it? The one whose client ended up driving to Oman when his cruise control got stuck going down the Al Ain Road?"

"Yes, that's Tom. Well, another client of his called him one evening last week from Al Hamra police station. 'I'm in a bit of bother here,' he told Tom, 'it's over a camel'. *Just what sort of trouble can you get yourself into over a camel?* Tom was wondering as he drove to the police station. But what you need to know about camels in the United Arab Emirates is they're highly revered animals and can sometimes be worth tens of thousands of pounds. They're used for racing and they even have their own beauty pageants. Harming one is a very serious matter indeed. Anyway, it turned out Tom's client was driving down the Emirates Road minding his own business when a camel wandered straight into his path. Collision was impossible to avoid and he hit the unfortunate creature head-on, knocking it off its legs and sending it sprawling across the bonnet of his car. When the camel came to rest, it was staring face-to-face through the windscreen at a very surprised client, its lips curled into a sneer and its eyes wild with fear."

"Wow! That must have been pretty scary for the guy."

"Very scary indeed, especially when the police turned up to arrest him. By that time, the camel had been carted off to the camel hospital for treatment and Tom's client had been told to pray for its survival. After several hours of wrangling by Tom and hand-wringing by his client, the client was eventually released on surrender of his passport, pending the possibility of the camel's owner coming forward to make a criminal complaint. The good news, though, is the camel lives on, so at least there'll be no need for blood money to change hands."

I'm waiting for all the questions that inevitably follow one of my Dubai stories, but instead Josh springs up and wraps his little arms tightly around my neck, drawing me in so we're cheek to cheek.

"Please take me and Margo with you when you go there," he says, a little too desperately for my liking. "I can share schools between here and Dubai, just like you share offices, and Margo won't mind either, really she won't."

This is about the other night, isn't it? The intruder, his tumble down the stairs, the night in hospital, Alex not believing his version of events. "I'd love that, Josh," I say, hugging him tighter, "but I'm not sure it's the solution. You can only go to one school at a time and, besides, dogs can't just jump on planes like us humans can, there's loads of procedures they need to go through first."

"Yeah, I suppose so," Josh says, pulling away from me to stroke Margo. "It's just that it's different when you're not here. Margo and me get bored being by ourselves all the time and I just think it would be much better if we went with you."

I think about how devastated Josh would be if he were ever separated from Margo. It's been a recurring niggle recently and one that I need to solve. Margo is one hundred percent Josh's dog – I'd been reluctant to take on the additional responsibility at first and Alex wasn't much bothered one way or the other, but Josh had lobbied us for months ('I'll walk it before and after school every day, and feed it and take care of it, you won't have to do a thing...') so eventually I'd relented. After all, without a brother or sister around and with me away so much of the time, Josh could do with the extra company. I didn't bother consulting Alex because this was something special I wanted to do on my own for Josh. It was a perfect summer's day last August when I'd bundled Josh into the car and we'd driven down the A3 to Guildford, to a dog breeder who specializes in beagles. And there was Margo, playing rough-and-tumble in a tri-coloured heap of puppies and looking far cuter in real life than in the photos I'd seen of her. By the time we'd got back home that day, the bond between boy and pup was already set as if by superglue and they've been inseparable ever since.

I want to pull Josh in again, to give him another hug, but he's still stroking Margo and watching me carefully, waiting for a response.

"Well, how about if I promise that by the time you're ten everything will have changed?"

And how the hell are you going to manage that, then?

"But that's ages away yet!"

Nope, it's next month, actually.

"Josh, it's only five weeks away, it will fly by, I promise. But in return you have to promise me to keep this our secret, okay?"

"Okay," says Josh, giving me a watery smile.

As I pull him back into a hug, my thoughts return to the dinner party tonight and I inwardly groan on Josh's behalf as well as my own. Alex thinks it's character building for Josh to mix with grown-ups, so he'll be expected to make an appearance downstairs for an hour or so before his bedtime. I know he hates these things as much as I do.

"You'd better get yourself changed into normal clothes, buddy, or the guests will be asking you for a karate demonstration. And remember, mum's the word," I say, giving Josh a wink and heading off for my shower.

The doorbell rings dead on eight o'clock as I'm making my way back downstairs. Alex will be cross I didn't make it down earlier to help out in the kitchen, but tough: Josh took precedence this evening. He's tight on my heels, changed into jeans and T-shirt, followed closely by Margo.

"I'll get it!" shouts Alex, dashing down the hallway to open the front door.

"It's *him*!" squeaks Josh as Alex lets in our first dinner guest.

My immediate thought is that Josh has spotted the rat from under our stairs – we've been after it for weeks.

"Where? Let's get him this time!"

"No, not the rat, the man. It's the guy who broke into the house the other night." Josh has buried his head into my back and is gripping me tightly around the middle. He sounds absolutely terrified. Margo is at his side and emitting a rare growl in our visitor's direction.

It's James O'Leary, I see, looking all fine and dandy in his cream linen suit, trench coat draped over the arm, fedora and walking cane in hand, like some kind of 1920s American movie star. Any lingering doubts about the identity of our intruder from the other night are instantly dispelled.

"Did I mention James is playing the lead role? Doesn't he look wonderful?"

Alex is actually gushing and it's mortifying.

"Absolutely!" I say as heartily as I can. "Just like *The Great Gatsby* himself!" *Except this isn't the Roaring Twenties in Long Island, USA, it's 2019 in Pimlico, London, and these are real lives you're wrecking* is what I'd like to add, but that would just come out sounding melodramatic so what I do say is, "Trying out a bit of method acting are we, James?" and I offer him my hand and look him up and down. "Actually, Josh thinks you look like the intruder who broke into our house last week whilst I was away in Dubai." I'm looking directly into his eyes as I say this: the shock is almost indiscernible, but it's there alright. He knows he's been rumbled. "You've never been here before though, right?" I continue. "So how could it possibly have been you?"

"That's right! Tonight is indeed my first visit to your beautiful home," he replies smoothly. "Besides, Gatsby's one of the good guys, isn't he?" I think this last bit's meant to be reassuring, because it's directed at Josh along with a slimy smile, but I can see by the look on Josh's face he's having none of it.

"Come on through to the lounge," says Alex, pulling James away from us. "I've got some absolutely divine bubbly for us to enjoy this evening."

Grrrr.

As Alex and James make their way through to the lounge, Josh is rooted to the spot at the bottom of the stairs and is staring at me as if I'm crazy for welcoming this brute into our home.

"Remember, you'll soon be ten," I tell him, tapping my nose. I wrap him in a tight hug and plant a kiss on the top of his head. I'm still feeling really shit about pretending not to believe him. He knows as well as I do it was James O'Leary letting himself into our house the other night, but what am I supposed to tell him? That I'm not enough for Alex?

And how long have I known about Alex's affair with James *bloody* O'Leary? About five years, I guess. I first discovered it a year or so after I'd started travelling to Dubai, but it could have been going on way before then for all I know.

It's a game we've been playing for years, Alex and I: I pretend Alex doesn't know that I know Alex is having an affair with James. Something like that – it's been a long thirty-six hours, but you get my drift.

This is getting far too close to home now, though, and it's harming Josh. We're way past the tipping point.

"Wait there, I'll be right back," I tell Josh, leaving him in the hallway and heading into the lounge after Alex and James. I bang the door closed behind me to protect Josh from what I've got to say.

"You," I snap, tossing my head towards James with as much disdain as I can muster, "are a cowardly piece of shit. You've obviously been sneaking in here for a quick shag after the show, taking full advantage of me being away and Josh being asleep, but this is *our* home, not *yours*."

"And *you*," I say, turning to Alex, "should be bloody ashamed of yourself, protecting a coward like him from of a nine-year-old. Your own son, for chrissakes!"

"But…"

"I don't want to hear it, Alex."

"…you're never here."

And there it is again: turning it all around and making it my fault.

They're both looking at me, waiting for my next move, but I decide not to get drawn in, there's no point. "Make sure he gives the bloody door key back before he leaves," I say, turning my back to them both and striding out of the room.

"Come on, let's get out of here," I say to Josh, who's sat on the stairs waiting for me. "How does pizza sound?" I say, and in that moment he looks as happy as I could ever wish him to be.

8.

Dubai
Eighteen days to Closing

Let me tell you how I know Samer Haddad: his son, a few months older than Noura and twice her size, is the nursery school bully. I've seen Haddad dropping him off at the classroom occasionally, a harassed maid running along behind them with the satchel and lunch bag. We exchange a 'good morning' if we cross paths but we've never really spoken. There's one particular occasion, though, that really sticks out in my mind. It was earlier this year – maybe around January or February time, when the weather was still cool enough to be outside during the day – and we were at a birthday party for one of the other kids from school. Amal and I were both there, along with most of the other parents from Noura's class. The grown-ups were congregated on the terrace, lounging on outdoor sofas and enjoying the bar service laid on for us by the birthday boy's parents, whilst Noura and her friends got to enjoy their own little party over by the swimming pool. A couple of entertainers, kitted out as Mickey Mouse and Snow White, were keeping them enthralled with a cute little show – magic tricks, juggling with skittles, balloon modelling, bubble blowing, that sort of thing. It all seemed to be going very well until a shriek of "HELP! HELP! GET ME OUT!" pierced the air, and then pandemonium broke loose. All the parents jumped to their feet and began running over to the kids; the kids were starting to cry, frightened by the scream and then by the mass panic of their parents; whilst Mickey Mouse and Snow White bolted off in the direction of the bouncy castle at the far end of the garden.

"WHAT THE HELL...?" This was from Haddad, who'd started legging it across the lawn in hot pursuit of Mickey Mouse and Snow White. For one crazy moment, I thought the Disney characters had bundled a child into one of their costumes and they were trying to make off with him. But then I noticed the bouncy castle. It wasn't looking right, sort of caved in on one side and sagging in the middle. It had been fine earlier, when the kids had been playing in it...

"FARIS! FARIS! I'M COMING TO GET YOU! DON'T PANIC." Haddad was now wading onto the flaccid castle right behind Mickey Mouse and Snow White, who were lifting a collapsed wall back into position and pulling Faris out from under it. The bottom half of the little boy's face was covered in a brownish-looking substance. Mud maybe, or something worse? Then Snow White bent down and retrieved what looked like a cowpat from the floor of the castle. On closer scrutiny, this turned out to be the squashed remains of a chocolate mousse cake. Faris Haddad had somehow managed to sneak it off the buffet table and away to the bouncy castle without being seen, and he was just getting tucked in when his hiding place had started to collapse around him. It transpired that Mickey Mouse had disconnected the electric air blower to the bouncy castle when he'd plugged in the bubble-blowing machine. Haddad went ape-shit, shouting about negligence and threatening to sue the birthday boy's parents for emotional distress. It was all very unfortunate.

Now here I am a few months later, busy in my office preparing to wrap up the Bailey's deal – along with my job in Dubai – and wondering how I'm going to get Haddad off my back. I've just received another text message from him:

Time is running out if we're going to do something about that personal dilemma of yours. Meet me at Starbucks, Emirates Towers mezzanine 11.30 today.

What does he think he knows about me, anyway? And how is any of it up for discussion? Even if he has somehow got wind of the fact I'm a bigamist, why meet at a coffee shop to discuss it? He's a creep and I'd prefer to keep ignoring him, but that tactic doesn't seem to be working so I put on my jacket and head over to Starbucks.

"So, Haddad," I say, taking the seat opposite him and placing my phone face-down on the table, "I got your cryptic messages. What's on your mind?"

"Good morning, Chris. Can I get you a coffee?"

I look at my watch. "No thanks," I tell him, "I can't stay long."

"Well, we'd better get straight to the point then, hadn't we?" says Haddad, slowly stirring his cappuccino. "Your boss Mark and I had an interesting little side discussion during that all-night meeting of ours."

He looks up at me at this point and raises his eyebrows as if waiting for me to respond.

"And?"

"Turns out you're married with a son back in London. Mark told me he and his wife attended your wedding a few years back and that your families still get together on a Sunday afternoon to walk the dogs in Hyde Park."

So there it is – the truth of my bigamist existence, fallen straight into the hands of an oily slimeball.

"Regent's Park, actually," I say. "Anyway, what of it?" My heart is banging in my chest and my throat has gone dry as a crispbread, but I'm determined to keep my voice steady.

"Well, you're also playing happy families here in Dubai with Amal and little Noura, aren't you? Want to explain to me just how that works, Chris?"

"That's none of your bloody business."

"That's just it, Chris, it very much is my *bloody* business. With the Bailey's Dubai deal going through in three weeks' time, I'm very concerned to discover that the lawyer on the other side of the deal is less than straight. 'Bigamy,' that's what it's called, isn't it?"

Here it comes then, the price to be paid for his silence. He seems to be enjoying this, the sadistic bastard, but if he's hoping for me to crumble or beg, he's going to be disappointed – I wouldn't give him the satisfaction.

"So, how shall we deal with this, Haddad?"

"I think we can help each other out here, Chris. We could have what you call a 'win-win' situation on our hands." He actually does that air quote thing with his index fingers at the 'win-win' part. It's nauseating. "It would be inconvenient, to say the least, if word got out about your 'bigamy'." There they go again, wriggling in the air – I feel like snapping them. "And think about how your two little families would react. Do you think either of them would want you after this?" He takes a sip of his coffee and licks his lips. "On the other hand," he continues, "it would be very convenient indeed if you failed to fulfil all of our due diligence requirements on the Bailey's deal. We'd have to talk about a reduced price then, wouldn't we?"

"What are you suggesting, exactly?"

"I'm suggesting you 'lose' all those ownership documents that you haven't yet produced."

He's talking about the conditional land assignment releases for the plots on which Mark's first six development projects are built. I found them this morning in one of the box files brought from store and I was in the middle of checking through them when I left to meet Haddad. I was planning to get them uploaded to the virtual data room this afternoon.

"Even if they were lost," I venture, "Mark will expect me to contact the master developers and banks and arrange duplicates."

"Yes, but how long would all that take? Weeks, if not months. Some of the master developers are out of business now, and banks have either merged or restructured. Al Shamsi would never agree to wait for you. You know how these businessmen are: it's always now, now, now. He'll want a quick, meaty price reduction to reflect the increased risk – at least twenty percent, I'd say – or he'll simply walk away."

Does Marwan Al Shamsi even know about this discussion we're having, I wonder, *or is this Haddad's own little game, angling for what he can get out of it for himself when the deal closes in Al Shamsi's favour?*

"The company does have clear title to those plots though, doesn't it?" Haddad's frowning when he asks me this, which makes me think this possible hitch in his grand plan has only just occurred to him. "If we find out after closing that Bailey's doesn't have clear ownership of those plots, I'll be making sure your bigamy gets the exposure it deserves."

What the hell am I going to do? My two kids need me, no doubt about that, and I have to find a way to look after them both once my role with Bailey's finishes. But can I really do this to Mark – sit by and see him tricked into selling his business for less than it's worth? Besides, Mark would never agree to it.

"Those releases are sat on my desk…"

Haddad holds up his hand to cut me off. "Before you reach any rash decisions," he says, "let me finish telling you why this is a deal you can't refuse. You see, I can make sure you're adequately compensated for your efforts. Shall we say five percent of the price reduction? Half a million dollars? As I said, this can be a 'win-win' situation."

When I see it, the perfect solution is so simple I almost laugh out loud. All the dangling ends that have been bothering me since Mark and Al Shamsi exchanged their contracts in that boardroom get instantly tied up into a beautiful golden bow.

"Okay, Haddad," I say, "we can consider those documents *lost*."

9.

Dubai
Seventeen days to Closing

"If I get SAMETA on board, my partnership's in the bag," says Tom, plucking a prawn out of his Pad Thai and popping it into his mouth. "Regular fees from the South African clients plus high-profile work with the Dubai government."

He's just returned from a four-day trip to Cape Town to attend his sister's wedding and whilst there he was invited along to a local SAMETA meeting to give a talk about doing business in the Middle East. The South African-Middle East Trade Association, Tom informs me, has a membership of several hundred businesspeople based across three cities: Johannesburg, Durban and Cape Town. Turns out they're all chomping at the bit to do business with the wealthy government agencies and enterprises of the Arab Gulf states. Some members are looking to capitalize on the growing food security concerns of the oil-rich but soil-poor Gulf nations by selling them South African farmland on which to grow their own sugar cane, fruit and vegetables, whilst others are keen to set up export channels for their gold, diamonds, platinum and minerals.

Understandably, Tom is keyed up at the prospect of having stumbled upon his own seam of gold. "It's a brilliant opportunity," he raves, "a once-in-a-lifetime thing. If it all goes well enough, my firm might even look at opening an office in Cape Town to channel the work back and forth. I'd be in charge of getting it set up and maybe I'll be able to spend more time down there on a regular basis. Wouldn't that be great?"

"Whoa, Tom! One step at a time!" I have to hand it to him, top marks for enthusiasm, but sometimes his ideas have a tendency to run away with him. "You've got to secure the SAMETA retainer first," I remind him. "These things can fizzle out to nothing, you know."

"Yar, but just think…"

To be honest, all I can think about right now is getting through the next three weeks, hopefully complete with my self-respect, a livelihood and two kids. I look at my watch: one-thirty already. I've got a meeting back at the office at two and Tom's got an urgent new shipping matter he needs to attend to. We've still got a lot of ground to cover in the next half hour so I just dive straight in. "Tom, how seriously do the Dubai authorities take white-collar crime?" I ask. "You know, bribery, fraud, that type of thing?" Tom knows this is about Haddad, that he's attempting to blackmail me, with a bit of bribery thrown in for good measure, all aimed at cheating Mark into selling his company cheap. We have no secrets, Tom and me. I've told him everything, and now I'm looking for his assurance that I'm doing the right thing. "They've really clamped down since the financial crisis, haven't they? You've been in Dubai for a good few years, so you must have some useful insight on the subject."

"You could say that," he replies. "After all, I was Aradiya's in-house legal counsel."

"Yes, I know. You've told me before," I say. "They were one of the real estate development companies that crashed during the financial crisis. You lost your job and went to work for Al Hattan."

"Yes, but that's not the full story of what went on there…"

Tom's looking around whilst he's telling me this and I find myself doing the same. The Financial Centre food court is a great place to sit and watch the world go by. Even Sheikh Mohammed and his entourage are known to pass through here from time to time on their way to the Capital Club or one of the more snazzy restaurants upstairs…*Shit, is that Amal over there? Coming down the escalators with Lubna?*

"By the time you started coming to Dubai in 2012," Tom's saying, "the city was already bouncing back to its old self: dynamic, ambitious, prosperous…"

Yikes, it is *Amal.*

"…but it had taken a huge amount of effort on the government's part to make that happen."

…with Lubna, looking like the bloody queen bee, as usual.

"First of all, they ushered in a raft of new laws and regulations to create a cleaner, more transparent environment to do business in…"

I'm trying to listen to Tom, to give him the attention his story deserves, but Amal has spotted me now and is coming over.

"It all went hand-in-hand with a state-led corporate witch hunt aimed at eradicating white-collar crime," Tom continues, clearly oblivious to my mounting horror. "Both the public and private sectors got a thorough royal cleanup…"

What the hell are Amal and Lubna doing here? This is where I work, not them. Their office is on the other side of Dubai – they're trespassing on my world. I know this sounds extreme, but nobody at the office knows about Amal and this food court is riddled with my work colleagues during the lunch hour. I've already spotted Naushad from accounts dashing past with an Express Curry takeaway and I'm pretty sure Dimple will be sat around here somewhere with her lunchtime buddies, clucking like hens over the latest tidbits of gossip.

"…and Aradiya was part of that."

I hope I'm nodding in all the right places, but it's an effort to focus on what Tom's saying with Amal making a beeline in our direction. What if one of my colleagues passes by and stops to be introduced? I can feel the threat of exposure bearing down on me like a ten-ton truck with each of those advancing Gucci-clad steps until Amal is right here, a towering presence at the side of our table.

"Not interrupting anything, are we?" is Amal's opening gambit, clearly intent on firing the first shot.

"No, not at all! What a pleasant surprise!" I reply, striving for the friendly tone that someone with nothing to hide would use with someone else who has nothing to hide. "This is Tom, a lawyer with Al Hattan. We're working together on a few things."

Amal takes Tom's proffered hand and gives it half a shake. "Good to meet you, Tom. And this is Lubna: we're also working together."

Touché.

"Anyway," I say, moving things along, "what brings you over to the Financial Centre? It's not your usual stamping ground."

"We've been viewing a retail unit that's just come up for rent on the mezzanine floor. We're thinking of opening a new Just Jewels store there," Amal explains.

"Plenty of bankers and lawyers with fat wallets and expensive women to please," adds Lubna, who's looking down her perfectly fixed nose at us in her usual imperious fashion. *"I've no doubt you've thoroughly tested the market from an end-user's perspective,"* is the response that's about to leave my lips when a far more pressing thought abruptly cuts in. "Aren't you supposed to be collecting Noura?" I ask Amal, snatching a look at my watch. "Nursery finished over an hour ago."

"Relax, I've got Rose doing it," says Amal dismissively. I hate it when Amal does this, fobbing the job off on to someone else – a child should be collected from school by a parent, not by a maid in a bloody taxi. "Anyway, we must run," Amal continues, unabashed. "Some of us have got work to do." And off they both go, their crisp robes flapping, taking the threat of my exposure away with them.

"So that's Amal?" says Tom, appraising the retreating figures.

"Yes, that's Amal. And the other one's Lubna Al Nuaimi. They grew up together and now they're business partners."

"Cosy." Tom's mulling this over, but we've got more important things to discuss and I need to bring the conversation back on track. "You were saying you were involved with a government crackdown whilst you were at Aradiya," I say. "Tell me what happened."

"It was an ordinary Sunday morning back in September 2009. I was sat in my office when the door to the reception burst open and the CID marched in. They rounded up all the senior execs, me included, and held us in one of the meeting rooms whilst they searched our offices and seized whatever they thought might help with their investigation."

I don't question Tom's innocence in all of this for a second, but innocent people get caught in the net all the time, casualties of the system, and the threat of it happening to you must be terrible. I wait for him to go on and finish the story.

"Turned out that for the past five years our CEO had been taking backhanders from sub-developers in return for cheap plots, and from construction companies in return for lucrative construction contracts. Nobody knows exactly how much he'd managed to squirrel away in offshore bank accounts over the years, but it certainly ran into the tens of millions. I had no idea he was crooked, he just didn't seem the type – a regular family guy, you know? In the end, he got fined twenty-five million dollars and sentenced to fifteen years' imprisonment followed by deportation. As you can see, the Dubai authorities take white-collar crime very seriously indeed."

"Okay, that's reassuring," I say, nodding. "So let's discuss how this is all going to work…"

And we use the remainder of our lunch break finalising a plan that involves some particular Somali 'businessmen' Tom is acquainted with over in Deira.

10.

Dubai
Fifteen days to Closing

There's not much going on in the office today: my work on the due diligence is done, all the quicker for me having 'lost' most of the outstanding documents, and the stuff I'd usually be working on, getting new property developments off the ground, is on hold pending Mark's sale of the company. Today's the day, then, to sort out the Cessna. According to Dimple's brother, Rajeev, the flight school in Fujairah is interested in doing a leasing deal with me but first I need to fly the plane up there for an inspection and test flight. A quick check of the weather reports and aviation notices online and I'm ready to go.

I can't make the trip without my flying buddy, of course, so I collect Noura from nursery and we head out to Al Maktoum airport together. It's predicted Al Maktoum will be bigger than Dubai International in a few years' time, maybe even the world's largest airport if Emirates moves its operations here as expected, but for now the air traffic in and out is relatively light and within the hour we're accelerating down Runway 30 for takeoff. Noura's sat next to me in her little booster seat, straining as far forward as she can get, her arms outstretched wide like the wings of a plane. This is her favourite part, and she giggles like mad as soon as we lift off the ground and nose up into the late-morning sky, made milky by moisture and dust.

Fujairah's on the east coast of the country and it will take us about an hour to get there. Five minutes into the flight and we're cruising at two thousand feet above sea level, putting behind us the glass-and-steel high-rises of downtown Dubai, the sprawling villa estates of well-heeled suburbia, made Floridian with their lakes and golf courses, then the industrial parks with their neat rows of warehouses, dully reflecting the bleached-out sky, and finally a labour camp where a cricket match is in full swing on the vacant building plot next door, until we've flown totally free of the city and all that lies ahead of us is an undulating expanse of terracotta sand, veined by roads and tracks and pot-marked by scrubby vegetation and ramshackle farm buildings.

There are a couple of restricted areas we have to navigate around and then I can settle back and relax into the flight. The first one is an absolute no-go area out near the Bab Al Shams desert resort – venture into it at risk of being escorted down by fighter jets. I go eastward to give that one a wide berth and spot below us a small thicket of trees I recognise: it's the site where we set up camp one weekend back in the winter when Noura and I joined a couple of other families on an overnight desert trip. Amal wasn't there, of course ('Me? Camping in the desert? I don't think so!' had been the response when I'd extended the invite) but Noura and I had a great time. I remember in the evening, way after the kids had gone to bed and us adults were sat around the campfire enjoying a nightcap, when an old Bedouin guy had appeared out of nowhere, camel in tow, and stood warming his hands by the fire. 'Salam alaykum,' he'd said, 'peace be upon you'. We replied with our alaykum as-salams, peace be upon you too, and then he slowly turned around and wandered off back into the blackness of the desert. When we told the kids about our night visitors the next morning, they didn't believe us until we showed them the camel's tracks in the sand. I go to point the site out to Noura, but she's fallen asleep beside me, lulled by the sound of the engine.

We're nearing the second restricted area now, the drop zone for the skydiving school out on the Al Ain highway, so I skirt around that before continuing north-east out over the desert toward the Hajar mountains.

This twenty-minute stretch between leaving the city and reaching the mountains is always the most relaxing part of the flight and I begin to feel the tension unloosening in my body. How wonderful it would be if we could do this every day, just Noura and me buzzing around the sky in our little plane. Actually, it was Noura's birth that set off the chain of events resulting in me owning the plane, so as far as I'm concerned we're equal partners in it. I'm not sure I'm ready to give that up.

Just think, if we continue for another fifteen minutes on this heading, we'll cross the border into Oman. Another hundred and seventy miles, and we'll be in Muscat…

I increase our altitude to four thousand feet and as we pass over the Hajar mountain range I feel the cord binding us to Dubai snap like an overstretched bungee, catapulting us forward towards something that feels like freedom. Noura's still sleeping soundly in the seat beside me as I turn the plane south, flying us down the coast toward Fujairah.

…On to Karachi, and from there we could just disappear. We're flying light, we could easily make it…

I let the idea settle on me, to see how it feels, like trying on a swanky outfit in a high-end fashion store your brain suspects you'll never wear but your heart says looks amazing on you.

...Sod Amal. And Haddad. I don't need to deal with these people.

I switch radio frequencies to make contact with Fujairah air traffic control.

"Fujairah approach. Alpha Six November Papa Charlie."

For a few moments I hear only static and then comes the reply, "Alpha Six November Papa Charlie. Go ahead."

"Four thousand feet. Approaching Khor Fakkan. Request amendment to flight plan to continue to Muscat."

"November Papa Charlie, confirm request to amend flight plan to divert to Muscat. Alpha Six November Papa Charlie."

"Affirmative. November Papa Charlie."

"November Papa Charlie, standby."

There, I've done it. We're on our way to freedom at last.

Nowadays, I can't even land in my own country without breaking out in a cold sweat, convinced I've been busted and the police are waiting to pick me up at passport control and whisk me away to Scotland Yard for questioning. The interview gets a regular rehearsal when I'm trying to fall asleep at night, a comedic parody of some clichéd ITV police drama that goes something like this:

BAD COP: A witness has come forward with evidence that you are married to both Alex Jones and Amal Al Zarouni. Is that correct?

ME: Erm...I suppose so.

BAD COP: You suppose so. Is that a 'yes' or 'no'?

ME: Well, yes then.

BAD COP: I'm not totally *au fait* with the legal system over in sunny Dubai, but here in Britain bigamy is a crime, punishable with up to seven years' imprisonment, a fine, or both. Do you understand?

ME: Yes, I'm a lawyer, it's my job to understand all that stuff. But I wasn't given much choice.

GOOD COP: Okay, let's start from the beginning. You married Alex here in London in May 2008. Is that correct?

ME: Yes.

GOOD COP: And your son, Josh, was born the following year.

ME: Is that a question?

BAD COP: Don't get smart with us, Chris. We're just trying to verify the facts here. Josh was born in July 2009, is that correct?

ME: That is correct.

GOOD COP: And you started travelling to Dubai in 2012. Is that right, Chris?

ME: That is right.

GOOD COP: So tell us when and where you met Amal.

ME: It was in the summer of 2014 at the Buddha Bar in Dubai Marina.

GOOD COP: And? Go on...

ME: Amal was there with a bunch of friends, celebrating the launch of a new fashion line by one of them. They were all Emiratis, but you wouldn't have known by the way they were casually dressed and guzzling champagne. Anyway, I was sat alone at the bar and Amal spotted me and brought me over a glass. One thing led to another...

BAD COP: And, hey presto! Before you knew it, you were a bigamist. Like to tell us how that happens, Chris?

ME: You have to understand I didn't set out to get married twice. It wasn't exactly an end goal of mine, like becoming a lawyer or a pilot. Sometimes, things happen that are outside your control and you just have to deal with them the best way you can. Have you ever done the wrong thing for all the right reasons?

BAD COP: We're not having a philosophical debate here, Chris. We're trying to get to the bottom of how you ended up having two families, one in London and the other in Dubai, and neither of them having a clue about the other.

GOOD COP: Most of us can't cope with one family. How do you manage with two of them? Two sets of household bills to pay, two sets of family holidays to arrange, two sets of in-laws to be nice to...

ME: Tell me about it! I deserve a bloody medal, if you ask me.

BAD COP: You don't get to decide what you deserve here, Chris. That's what the criminal justice system is for. To punish criminals like you.

ME: Ouch.

GOOD COP: This needn't be painful. Just tell us in your own words how you got yourself into this situation. Cooperate with us fully, and I'm sure we can persuade the CPS to go easy on you.

ME: Well, it all started when I found out Alex was having an 'inappropriate relationship', let's call it, with James *bloody* O'Leary. Can you believe it? There was me, slogging my guts out between London and Dubai, working around the clock to do the best for my family, torturing myself with a diet and exercise regime fit for an Olympic athlete just to ward off the constant jet lag, and there was Alex, living the life of blooming Riley back home and fooling around with James *bloody* O'Leary.

GOOD COP: You must have felt very shocked when you found out. I would have been devastated myself.

ME: It was a real slap in the face, but Josh was only five at the time and I was working away from home three days out of seven. What was I supposed to do? Splitting up the family wasn't an option as far as I was concerned. I decided to put up with it.

BADCOP:SoyougotevenbymarryingAmal?Thatwasyour solution?

ME: No, that was accidental. Completely unintentional.

BAD COP: I can't wait to hear it.

ME: It started out as just an affair. A way of getting even with Alex, sure, but also to add some excitement to my life. And somehow the fact it was happening in a country far away from home made it feel less real, more like a fantasy, and therefore not such a bad thing.

GOOD COP: Affairs happen all the time, nothing criminal in that, Chris. Not in this country, anyway. I don't know about Dubai...

ME: Well, the laws over there are a bit weird when it comes to...

BAD COP: My partner wasn't asking you for a lecture on Shari'ah law, smart ass. You're in Great Britain now. There's no harm in having an innocent little fling as far as we're concerned, but you didn't stop at that, did you? You just had to push it all the way. Nice intimate little wedding ceremony on the island of Cyprus, I gather. All very romantic.

ME: Is that a question?

BAD COP: Don't start with me again. Just tell us how you got there.

ME: Emirates. They fly daily to Larnaca.

GOOD COP: I think what my partner is asking is: why did you marry Amal when you were already married to Alex, when you knew it was a crime and that if you were ever caught you would lose everything – the people you love, your career, your freedom...

ME: Okay, I'll tell you and then you'll see that I had no choice. One morning Amal was rushing to get me to the airport in time for a flight and was driving much too fast down the Sheikh Zayed Road. We crashed into the central barrier and the car flipped over onto its roof, bringing Noura into the world later that day, three and a half months premature. No one else knew about the pregnancy. In fact, an abortion was scheduled for the following week and if that had gone ahead, everybody could have gone about their lives none the wiser. But suddenly there she was, a beautiful little girl who was meant to be born. At that point, I had no choice but to marry Amal. Having a child outside of marriage is a serious crime in Dubai, and we had Amal's family breathing down our necks, telling us to do the right thing. I didn't tell them I was already married – how could I? That would just have made matters worse. Before we knew it, we were put on a plane to Cyprus to arm ourselves with a marriage certificate, what Amal called our 'stay-out-of-jail card', which got backdated twelve months upon its translation from Greek to Arabic to cover up our daughter's illegitimacy.

BAD COP: The Al Zarounis, they're one of the oldest, wealthiest families in Dubai, aren't they? Sounds as if you landed on your feet out there, living it up in the lap of sunny luxury.

ME: Hardly! I have a full-time job to do, you know. When I'm there, I'm working. When I'm here, I'm working. If I'm not working, I'm running backwards and forwards trying to keep everyone happy. It's a constant struggle, keeping it all going. I'd like to see you try to manage it. You wouldn't last a week...

GOOD COP: Shall we take a break? I'll get you a nice cup of tea.

And that's where my imaginary interview trails off and I'm brought back to the real world. I wonder what those two police officers would make of me flying around like this in my own plane with Noura by my side? Bad Cop would have a field day with that one. How my new in-laws wanted to buy Amal and me a villa in Jumeirah as a wedding gift, but I declined as I felt more at home staying in my own place, so how they bought us matching Bentleys instead, a nod to my British heritage, and how I sold mine to buy the Cessna, sharing my childhood dream with my precious daughter. I suppose Bad Cop would say it's all a bit far-fetched.

This is a ridiculously easy way to get Noura out of the country and, quite honestly, Amal would hardly notice she's gone. But there's also Josh to consider, Noura's big brother, thousands of miles away but just as important. I can't do this, can I? I have to stick to the original plan. I radio in to Fujairah approach again, "November Papa Charlie. Cancel request for amended flight plan. Intention to continue to Fujairah as filed."

"November Papa Charlie, continue inbound. Descend two thousand feet. Report abeam container port."

"Descend two thousand. Report abeam container port. November Papa Charlie."

I pull back on the throttle to start our descent toward Fujairah airport and our day progresses in line with my original objectives: the flight school agrees to take a ten-year lease on the plane, at sufficient rent to cover its overheads and provide a surplus income on top. Noura and I leave our plane in its new hangar and catch a lift back to Dubai with one of the instructors.

When we arrive home, my maid and mother-in-law both come running down the corridor at us, frantic. I should have told them I was taking Noura out of nursery for the day, so I apologise. What can I say? That I wish we didn't need their help, that I actually resent them for it? They take Noura out of my arms and whisk her away for bath time and bed and I'm left bereft in the hallway with a flight to Heathrow to catch. My bag is packed from this morning, ready to go. When it attacks like this, the loneliness feels dreadful.

11.

London
Fourteen days to Closing

The dazzling Pan Am-esque vision of air travel that fuelled my dreams as a kid growing up on a council estate in Bristol has since faded well and truly to grey. I still love piloting my own plane, but having clocked over eight hundred trips back and forth to Dubai during the last few years, each of them three thousand four hundred miles and nearly seven hours long – that's a whopping two million, seven hundred and twenty miles and two hundred and thirty-three days! – I'm no longer a happy passenger. Each flight seems to stretch out that little bit longer, feel that tad more oppressive. I'm no Tom Ford or Narendra Modi either, one of those 'sleepless elite' capable of functioning on three or four hours' kip a night – I need my full eight hours to function as a normal human being – so this red-eye flight to Heathrow is particularly brutal. After endless hours of enforced shut-eye prostrate on a not-quite-flat bed, breathing in stale cabin air and listening to the big guy across the aisle from me bellowing like a prize bull, I'm less than ready for the full day at the office ahead of me. Landing at Heathrow was a particularly bleak affair this morning – grey overcast skies, air misty with drizzle – but I wasn't arrested at passport control, so silver linings and all that. And I spied a blue patch of sky opening up through the clouds as the cab turned into my street just now, so the day might just be looking up.

I've had a long journey home and I'm looking forward to the embrace of familiarity when I let myself in through my front door. Eight o'clock on a school day so Josh will be at the kitchen table, more or less dressed in his grey and maroon uniform, spiky bedhead hair still in need of a damp down, and tucking into his scrambled eggs with Marmite on toast; Margo will be nosing her food bowl noisily across the kitchen floor, wolfing down her meat and biscuits before it gets whisked away and she's put out in the back garden until the humans are ready to leave the house; Alex will be busy preparing Josh's packed lunch, dressed to the nines for the school run and chatting along to *Good Morning Britain* or whatever it is they show on breakfast television these days.

These are all the things I expect to see happening when I let myself in through the front door of my Victorian terraced home. Instead, there's silence. I drop my bags in the hallway and shrug off my jacket, hanging it on the rack next to Josh's blue parka. Has he gone off to school without it again? The number of times I've nagged him to wear it. The house feels cold and a chill runs down my spine. Margo trots down the hall to greet me, wagging her tail. "Where's everybody, eh girl?" I ask, but she just wags her tail harder, happy to see someone. I follow her into the kitchen, turning on the lights as I go to chase away the gloom, and she stops to inspect her food and water bowls. They're both empty and gleaming with cleanliness. That's a worry: Josh wouldn't forget to feed Margo her breakfast before going off to school. I open the back door to let her out into the garden and fill up her water bowl from the kitchen tap. Last night's dinner dishes are still soaking in the sink and I pull out the plug to drain away the greasy water.

I'll just give Alex a call and see where they are.

But all I get is voicemail: *Sorry, I can't take your call right now as I'm off doing something fabulous! Chat later! Hasta la vista, baby!*

"What the hell are you doing that's so fabulous at eight o'clock on a Thursday morning when you're supposed to be getting our son off to school?" That's the message I'd like to leave, but I decide "Alex, call me," would be more conducive to a quick response.

Hanging up, I make my way upstairs. I sense before I see that Josh's bedroom is empty, his bed neatly made up and the curtains open. In contrast, our bedroom – yes, the one I still share with Alex, keeping things 'normal' – is in darkness, curtains closed tight against the daylight. There are two human-sized mounds under the duvet and relief sweeps through me. Josh has spent the night with Alex and they've both overslept. Thank God! I go to wake them up but as I approach the bed, I see Alex spooning against a body that's much larger than Josh's, a body with a large head attached to it, a head that's sprouting a messy thatch of dirty blond hair, greasy with stale pomade.

What the...

Alex's bed buddy isn't Josh at all. It's James *bloody* O'Leary. This is sodding *déjà vu*. Rewind five years and I'm sat in an office in Warren Street explaining to Ms. Belinda Potts, PGDip, BACP, how I discovered my marriage was a sham.

"I bet you hear these stories all the time, don't you? It's all mundane stuff until the day it happens to you. Then it shatters your world like a crystal vase smashed into a wall. I need to find a way to put it all back together again, to keep going on," I'd told Ms. 'please call me Belinda' Potts. To her credit, she hadn't looked too fazed by this challenge. "Let's just start right at the beginning, Chris," she'd said. So I'd told her the whole story of Alex and me, from when we'd first met right up until James *bloody* O'Leary had entered the frame.

"It was back when I was a trainee solicitor and working as a photographer in my spare time to bolster my salary. I'd found a niche line of work with an agency in Piccadilly specialising in live events photography, and I'd been hired by a West End theatre company to take the photos for the program of their upcoming show. Alex was one of the cast, and at the end of the session had asked if I was available over the next few weekends to shoot some personal portfolio shots in various locations across London. So that's what we did: I shot vintage Alex in Carnaby Street, sophisticated Alex sat at the bar of some high-end jazz club, domesticated Alex flying a kite in the park with a borrowed child and dog as props, even a black-clad Alex in mourning at some unfortunate soul's graveside.

"I still look at those portfolio shots as my best-ever work. Alex is very photogenic, actually, a real natural – great body, elegant styling, a face that can transform instantly to fit any setting, all very seductive... God, I've been a gullible idiot, haven't I?"

"Just tell the story, Chris," Belinda had prompted, "and then we'll talk about some coping mechanisms for those negative feelings."

So I told Belinda how, over the course of those first few weeks, our relationship came out from behind the camera and turned into friendship, how our weekend 'shoots' became more like dates and how before long we were an 'item'. I told her how we were just starting out in our respective careers, both only twenty-two and equally ambitious for ourselves: I wanted to be a hot-shot corporate lawyer and Alex wanted to make it big in film.

"It was a case of *opposites attract*," I told her. "More *opposite* than *attracted* as it turns out, but I'm getting ahead of myself." I explained how we talked about going to New York: I'd qualify with the New York bar and Alex would aim for Broadway, en route to Hollywood. And how it didn't work out that way. I had been identified as a 'rising star' early on with Coulters, and got promoted to associate and given a client list as soon as I qualified as a solicitor. A quick succession of promotions, largely thanks to Mark Bailey's loyalty to me, got me a junior partnership by 2008, and all grown up we decided to get married. I explained how Alex had yet to land a lead role and how any ambition in that direction was slowly fading away. But that was okay, because Josh came along the following year and now Alex had a new purpose in life. My career had continued to soar whilst Alex stayed at home. I told her how our lives started to diverge and how my travelling to Dubai, when it had begun two years before, had served to drive the wedge between us even deeper.

"And then, three weeks ago I got home earlier than expected from Dubai. It was late morning when I reached the house, and Josh was at school. I let myself in and noticed a blue wool overcoat I didn't recognise on the bannister. I made my way upstairs and opened the bedroom door to be confronted by the sight of James *bloody* O'Leary humping away on top of Alex. I reversed my steps out of the bedroom, down the stairs and out the front door and took myself and my wheelie case to the pub for want of a better place to hang out until the coast was clear. Two vodka-and-tonics later I'd resolved to keep my knowledge of Alex's affair to myself: breaking up our family unit is not the best thing for Josh, especially with me being away so much of the time and Alex becoming less and less responsible. So here I am, talking to you in the hopes of finding a way to deal with Alex's betrayal whilst pretending everything's normal for Josh's sake."

Belinda was great, actually. I ended up having three or four sessions with her and she really helped me to cope with my harsh new reality. It was when I was coming out of that process I first met Amal, and you know where that got me: into a whole heap of other trouble. I really ought to have listened to my therapist when she told me not to go looking for payback. Anyhow, that's going to get resolved for better or for worse within the next two weeks. Right now I have a more pressing concerns:

Where the hell is Josh?

That first time five years ago when I'd found Alex sharing our bed with O'Leary I'd made a hasty retreat and gone down the pub to regroup. This time I have no choice but to force myself further into the bedroom. A ball of nausea rises up my chest and into my throat as I approach the bed and give Alex's shoulder a rough shake, trying to get some response. The all-familiar stench of stale alcohol assails me as Alex rolls over towards me.

"Where's Josh, Alex? He's not in his bed." I'm right up close to Alex's ear, but nada: Alex just mumbles and rolls back over to spoon against our half-welcomed interloper. I'm wasting my time here, and I need to get out, fast.

I exit the bedroom and search the rest of the house and garden. I call the school. No, Josh hasn't turned up for class today. I'm refusing to panic just yet, despite a familiar feeling of fatalism that's welling up, telling me this was always going to happen. My dark angel, at it again. I call our babysitter. She had a Uni event on yesterday evening, so couldn't come over when Alex had rung last night. Apparently, it was the last night of *The Great Gatsby* and Alex was planning to go to the after-show party. The evidence in the bedroom upstairs certainly bears this out. Bloody brilliant! Not even a member of the cast, but Alex has to be there, hanging out at every available opportunity, desperate to be part of the scene even though there hasn't been a role to play for years, besides serving as O'Leary's lovesick muse, that is.

Where else can I look? Who else can I phone? If the babysitter wasn't available last night, perhaps Josh went for a sleep-over with one of his mates instead?

But that doesn't explain why he's not in school today…

I'm scrolling through my contacts ready to start calling round parents of school friends when the phone on the kitchen wall pierces the silence with its 1970s trill.

"I've only gone and found your bloomin' dustbin lid down 'ere at the playhouse, aven't I! Would you Adam an' Eve it? Left on a pile of old curtains back of the stage."

I immediately recognize the voice with its heavy Cockney accent: it's Reggie, the caretaker down at the theatre. But he must be confused. I haven't owned a dustbin with a lid since the council supplied us with wheelie bins years ago, and even if I did have a dustbin lid, what would it be doing at the theatre?

"Reggie, that's very kind of you to let me know, but I'm pretty sure it's not my lid so maybe you need to ask around a bit more."

I'm about to thank Reggie and hang up when I hear him say something quite startling:

"I know your lad when I see him, alright, and I'm telling you it's 'im. Proper Hank Marvin 'e is as well."

"You've found Josh, Reggie? Oh, thank God! I'll be right there."

Josh and Reggie are waiting for me outside the theatre when I get there ten minutes later. Josh is leaning against the wall, head down and looking thoroughly dejected. What nine-year-old wouldn't be after the appalling night he's just had? Getting dragged to a raucous after-show party to watch your 'responsible parent' getting pissed along with everyone else, and waking up the next morning locked up alone in a theatre when said parent took lover-boy O'Leary home instead of you at the end of the night? (Okay, so Josh doesn't know about that last bit, thank God, and I intend to keep it that way.)

Time to take my *Hank Marvin dustbin lid* – or 'starving kid', as I've worked out during my trip over here – for a bit of refuelling and TLC.

"Reggie, thank goodness you found him," I say, getting out of the taxi and pulling the old guy into a brief hug. "I've been going out of my mind with worry. I owe you one."

"Right you are," he says, blushing with the fuss of it all. "I'd best be getting 'ome to the trouble and strife."

I watch Reggie amble down the street. *What a nice bloke*, I think. *Just the type of man you'd want as your dad.* Instead, my dad had taken off when I was Josh's age, leaving me to cope with a young brother and a depressed, alcoholic mother who extracted far more from her kids than could ever be considered healthy, even back in the eighties when children were less coddled than they are today. I don't bear any grudges, though – it catapulted me out of that council estate and into a decent profession. I've achieved things that were never mine to achieve, things that belonged to other sorts of people ('imposter syndrome' Belinda had once called it). *Whatever, I want a much better childhood for my kids.*

"I'm really sorry," Josh is saying, "I got tired waiting to go home so I found a pile of old curtains to sleep on. I didn't mean to get locked in and it was so dark and scary." Josh is on the verge of tears and I don't blame him: Alex's treatment of our son is getting more brutal with each passing week.

"Come on, let's go to Micky's for breakfast and sort all this out," I say, taking his hand and leading him up the street. Micky's is our local greasy spoon café and it serves a wicked full English breakfast with proper builders tea in chipped enamel mugs. Alex wouldn't be seen dead in the place, which just makes it all the more appealing for Josh and me when we're looking for somewhere to escape to for a while.

"Just remember what I promised you: everything will have changed by the time you're ten," I tell Josh once we're comfortably settled at a corner table and waiting for our food.

"Are you sure you're not just saying that to make me feel better?" Josh says. "Because I hate everything right now. I'm scared when you're not at home to look after me."

"I know, but have I ever lied to you? I made you a promise and I'm going to keep it. You'll be ten before you know it and in the meantime, how about we head up to the high street after breakfast and buy you a mobile phone? Strictly for emergencies, mind. Then you'll just need to call me if ever you're in trouble again."

Apparently this is a brilliant interim solution because Josh's face instantly lights up like a Belisha beacon.

I just hope whenever he needs to call me on that phone, I'll be there to help him.

12.

Dubai
Eleven days to Closing

It seems that after a five-year hiatus, the Somali pirates are at it again, and Tom's been called in to help get one particular merchant vessel and its unfortunate crew released.

"It's a highly lucrative and organized business," Tom explains as we make our way along the quayside towards our meeting point. "The pirates are generally just ordinary local fishermen with impoverished families to feed and a livelihood threatened by illegal foreign fishing trawlers. They're usually part of a larger, sophisticated investment syndicate that arms and equips the pirates and handles the ransom payment. It's just like a business venture. Some participants, such as the investors, the pirate crew and their leaders, are issued 'A' shares in the venture, which gives them a percentage of the eventual ransom payment, whilst other participants such as armed guards, interpreters and middlemen get 'B' shares, which entitle them to a fixed success fee. So when a vessel is taken hostage, the pirates know exactly how much ransom money they need to demand to make sure everyone involved gets paid their proper amount."

"And in this case, they're demanding three million dollars for the release of MV *Azusa*, right?"

"Yep, and after two months we've only managed to raise one million, all from charitable donations. But I reckon the pirates will be ready to settle at that amount by now. They know the ship owner doesn't have any money – it's all tied up in the boat and its cargo – and the Sri Lankan crew don't have any wealthy relatives to help out, so where else will the money come from? The pirates should have chosen an Emirati-owned vessel with a Pakistani crew; that would have got them a full payout, for sure. Anyway, I've taken the risk of depositing the one million with the hawala agent this morning. If they agree to settle at that amount, we can get this over and done with today."

This side of the Dubai Creek is unfamiliar territory to me. Being down here at the old dhow wharf and looking back across the choppy waters to see the Burj Khalifa and her surrounding high-rise sisters glinting in the middle distance gives me a feeling of being cut off from my world, a spectator looking in from the outside. We've crossed Al Maktoum Bridge and taken a step back in time, maybe by fifty years, even a hundred years. Dozens of creaking wooden dhows line the quayside, three or four deep in some places, their flat decks laden with tarpaulined cargo heaped amongst displays of unexpected salty domesticity as lines of washing flap in the breeze and cooking pots boil up the lunch. Wiry men in stained T-shirts and ankle-length lungis busy themselves loading and unloading their pallets of cigarette cartons, car tyres, air conditioning units, televisions and washing machines, bikes and mopeds, all on their way around the Arabian Gulf and Indian Ocean to be dropped off and picked up at their various locations: Iran,

Iraq, Pakistan, India, Oman, Somalia. It's a minor miracle such an old maritime tradition has survived in the heart of this twenty-first-century city.

All this time Dimple has been dawdling along behind Tom and me, off in her own little selfie world. I hope she can swim because she's awfully close to the water's edge and I've no wish to go jumping in after her if she topples off.

"Dimple, keep up. This isn't a photography tour, you know."

"Isn't Dubai amazing!" she exclaims, putting on a quick spurt to catch us up. "You know they're developing a Bubble City that will float over us like a huge balloon?"

"No, I can't say I was aware of that." I look over at Tom, who shrugs and gives a shake of his head. This is clearly news to him as well.

"How do you think they're going to do that, Dimple?" he asks.

"They're going to make it out of special bendy glass and power it with two zillion solar panels. They're going to put theme parks and hotels inside…you know, for all the tourists and whatnot. Think of how much AC they'll need to keep it cool in the summer!"

I think both Tom and I have twigged what's going on here.

"And where did you hear about this, Dimple?" I enquire.

"It was on Twitter this morning."

"Ah yes, and was it from the Pan-Gulf Echo by any chance, Dimple?"

"Precisely! So it's really happening, isn't it?"

"You do realize the Pan-Gulf Echo is a satirical publication, don't you?"

"Of course I am knowing this!" Dimple gives her head a gentle shake of gratitude for its unwavering wisdom. "It writes about all the controversial stuff that goes on that nobody else has the guts to publish."

"Erm, not quite," Tom chips in. "It takes things that are really happening in the region that are a little bit unbelievable and then exaggerates them to make them funny. It's all fake news," he says, giving her a wink and letting it all sink in.

The shocked realization that crosses Dimple's face causes her eyes to grow wide, but her look of surprise gets quickly displaced by a disappointed frown.

"You mean we're not actually meeting with pirate negotiators this morning?"

"No, that's all true, Dimple," Tom reassures her.

"Thank goodness, because this is going to be very interesting indeed."

I'm beginning to regret my decision to bring Dimple along, but she was so excited when I'd told her where Tom and I were going this morning, plus she could do with a break from searching for all those 'lost' documents. Okay, so I was feeling a tad bit guilty, but hopefully she can make herself useful as well; go and get sandwiches if the negotiations drag on, take notes, those sorts of assistantsy things.

We stop on the quayside adjacent to an old wooden dhow. "This is the one," Tom confirms, pointing to the name painted in black italics on the ship's prow. *Heaven's Treasures*. There's no one around as we step aboard, but the hatch to the lower deck is open and we make our way down the steps, calling out our tentative *salam alaykums* as we go. In the dim light of the cabin, I make out three men sat at a galley table. They're mature looking, perhaps in their early sixties, all sporting greying goatees and dressed uniformly in white open-collared shirts and suits in varying shades of brown. These Somali 'businessmen' are the Dubai face of the syndicate behind the taking of MV *Azusa*.

"Alaykum as-salam," says the one nearest us, rising to his feet. There's no offer of a hand for shaking, I notice. Instead, he indicates we should take a seat on the bench across from them. Once we're settled, he clicks his fingers and a galley hand dressed in a ragged khamiis hobbles over to pour tea into three small cups from one of those tall Arabic-style teapots. Whilst the Somalis watch silently from across the table, we take tentative sips of the steaming sweet tea until we drain our cups and place them down, giving them a shake in customary fashion to indicate we've had enough. *Shukran*, we say. Thank you. With these formalities out of the way, discussions can begin.

"Mr Tom, we have missed you. It has been too long since our last meeting," says the Somali in the middle, with no trace of a smile and a tone I'd describe as wooden. "And since you have brought your friends with you, I assume we will have cause to celebrate this time," he says, without taking his eyes off Tom. "The alternative scenario would indeed be most unfortunate."

I rapidly revise my assessment of this guy. He's not wooden – he's downright bloody threatening. He's smaller than the other two, I see, and is wearing tinted steel-framed glasses and a gold Rolex. This one's the boss, that's for sure.

Tom introduces Dimple and me as his 'colleagues' and brings the conversation round to business.

"The bottom line is that you picked the wrong boat."

Just like that, Tom's out with it. But is his blunt opening gambit going to secure him a stronger hand in the negotiations with our stony hosts or will it merely serve to piss them off? It's a gutsy call, I'll give him that.

"And *you*," growls the third Somali, the one we haven't heard from yet, "picked the wrong people to mess with." His enunciation is slow and thick, much like his intelligence, I suspect. The Boss raises his hand a notch to command silence and the effect on his two flunkeys is immediate as they shrink down into their seats.

"You seem to misunderstand us," says the Boss. "We didn't orchestrate any of this. Do you really think we'd make such a basic mistake, taking the most pitiful boat on the Indian Ocean hostage? No, no, no, Mr Tom. That's not it at all."

"Then please enlighten us, sir," says Tom, "because the last time we met you were demanding three million dollars for the release of the *Azusa*."

"Not us, Mr Tom, no. We are merely helping out our fellow countrymen, simple men of the sea who are trying to earn a living in the best way they know how, to support their starving wives and children. There is nothing in this for us, Mr Tom. This is our Zakat, our charitable assistance."

Dimple lets out a tut at this and shuffles with displeasure. I give her a sharp look. She had her instructions before coming aboard: just smile pleasantly and don't say a word. Honestly, it's not that difficult.

"That's very generous of you, sir," says Tom, not missing a beat. "And we will try to match your generosity with our own *final* offer of financial assistance, made possible by the generous donations of the kind community here in the UAE."

With this, Tom puts his hand in his jacket pocket and pulls out a folded piece of paper. He places it on the table in front of him and pushes it towards our hosts. The flunkey with the suspect intelligence snatches it up and hands it to his boss. I'm holding my breath as the Boss unfolds the piece of paper and absorbs the figure scrawled across it.

"Please take more tea whilst we see what we can do," says the Boss rising from his seat.

The three Somalis make their way through a low doorway at the back of the galley, which presumably leads onto the bridge. I guess from there they can make radio contact with their compatriots sat on the *Azusa* waiting to hear word.

"Looks like your intuition was right, Tom," I say. "That was all just face-saving, wasn't it, all that stuff about not making a basic mistake themselves, that they're just trying to help people back home?"

"Yeah, I think so. It must be pretty clear to everyone involved by now they made the wrong call when choosing the *Azusa* to take hostage. They've rung it out as much as they can. But let's just sit tight and see. These things are hard to predict."

The excitement I can hear in Tom's voice is there with good reason: he's told me that the SAMETA account is already secured, and if he can settle this case as well his partnership with Al Hattan is in the bag.

My phone pings with a message and I pull it out of my pocket, intending to just put it on silent. But the message is from Haddad. *What does he want now?* I tap on his name and an image of Josh and me fills the screen. It's from the café the other day, where we went to have breakfast after I'd picked him up from the theatre. I'm instantly choked up. Josh is looking at me with such misery and longing, with such utter dependency to which I'm yet to feel entitled. '*Happy Families No. 1*,' is the accompanying message. Bloody Haddad, he's got people stalking me now! He's collecting evidence in case I renege on his sleazy deal. A second message suddenly appears and I scroll down, scanning as I go, '*Marwan Al Shamsi wishes to meet you...to discuss ongoing business...Come to his office at 10.00 am on Tuesday.*'

"Everything okay, Chris?" Tom's looking at me with a very concerned expression.

"Just more of the usual." I send a reply, '*confirmed*', and slip the phone back in my pocket. I give Tom a reassuring wink and turn my attention to Dimple. She's fully absorbed with her phone, probably uploading her earlier selfie efforts on to her Facebook page.

At this juncture, the flunkey without the handshake half emerges through the doorway from the bridge and beckons us to follow him.

"The captain of the MV *Azusa* has something to say to you," the Boss tells Tom when we join them, and he hands him the transceiver handset.

To hear over the dhow's radio from the MV *Azusa*'s reinstated captain that the pirates have finally vacated the vessel by skiff and scooted off across the waters back in the direction of the Somali coast is truly a wonderful moment. Dimple is beaming from ear to ear and bouncing with the effort of not speaking. Meanwhile, Tom is maintaining a neutral air as he reaches into his shirt pocket and pulls out a second folded piece of paper. The password. That's all the Somalis need to give to the hawala agent in Mogadishu in return for one million dollars cash, paid out across the counter to the syndicate's representative. Tom hands the password over to the Somali boss, who reads it and shakes his head, his face inscrutable.

As we leave the dhow and step back onto the quayside I can't help but ask the question that's been bugging me for the last few minutes.

"Just out of interest, Tom, what was the password?"

He finally allows himself a grin. "Wanker," he replies.

13.

Dubai
Ten days to Closing

By the time I arrive at my in-laws' house (the Dubai ones, that is, not the other ones from Surrey), their back garden is already teeming with guests and the party's in full swing. I spot Amal's father over by a gift-laden trestle table chatting with two other white-robed men, neighbours maybe or business acquaintances, and I curse myself for coming empty-handed. A month of Sundays could come and go before it would occur to Amal to pick up a gift. *Bugger, I should have sent Dimple out to get something this afternoon.* What symbolises forty-five years of marriage, anyway? Silk? Crystal? Lace? Coral? Ball-and-chain, perhaps? Or, in my case, one of those Zoom Balls we all had as kids, except I'd be the ball that's sent zipping backwards and forwards on the strings, running between my two spouses. Good on the Al Zarounis, I suppose: if you can hold it together for that long, it's actually a humongous gold medal you deserve. Even with the doubling up I've done, I'll only have scraped together a total of fourteen years of wedlock by the time all this is over.

God, I'm starving! I haven't eaten anything since breakfast, and that was only a banana smoothie before dashing out the door. It's been an extra busy day of phone calls and emails, getting ready for life after closing, and now it's gone nine o'clock. *Maybe I can grab a quick plateful from the buffet whilst my mum-in-law's still showing Noura off to the neighbours?*

"Chris, my dear, you're here!"

Nope, too late. Amal's mother breaks away from her gaggle of friends and wafts over to greet me, sprinkling a dose of glamour and sophistication with every step she takes in her crystal-spangled kaftan, a lavish take on the traditional plain black abaya. Noura's tottering along by her side dressed in a chiffon creation alarmingly similar to her grandmother's. Fatima had begged to choose Noura's dress for this evening – 'Please, let's get her out of those jeans and T-shirt and let her be a proper girl for once,' she'd said – with the result I can hardly recognize my own daughter. But this Mini-Me thing Fatima's got going on is just the tip of the iceberg.

I sweep Noura up into a hug, plant a kiss on her cheek and take a look around. A huge Bedouin marquee has been set up in the Al Zarounis' back garden with layers of Persian silk rugs lining the floor, festoons of ruby red and deep burgundy sheer voile drapes billowing gently in the night-time breeze, and ornate Moroccan chandeliers sparkling crystal gold overhead. *Bloody hell, we've got Arabian Nights on steroids going on here.* One corner is set up with floor cushions and shisha pipes, whilst in the opposite corner a whole goat is sizzling on a spit over a charcoal fire, flanked on either side by the predictably laden trestles of food I'd clocked earlier: bowls of baba ganoush, fattoush salad, tabbouleh, falafels, lamb koftas, shish taouk, manakeesh and flatbreads, with dessert of umm ali, kunafeh and whole fruits.

"Amal will be here soon," I say to Fatima. "You know what the traffic can be like from the airport." I'm wondering why I should bother apologizing on Amal's behalf to a long-suffering mother who knows her child only too well when Amal walks through the gate arm-in-arm with Lubna, the pair of them wrapped up in each other's company and giggling like schoolgirls.

"Speak of the devil," I mutter. Fatima glances in my direction and quickly away again, no doubt reading my mind all too clearly, before rushing over to greet the mirthful couple.

It's been like this since I first met Amal in the Buddha Bar six years ago. There'd been a group of Emirati friends there that night, but only one of them stands out in my memory. Sodding Lubna. I don't even know to this day who all the others were. Lubna had come across the room when she'd spotted Amal talking to me and had wrapped a languid arm around Amal's neck, asking to be introduced.

"This is Lubna," Amal said, giving Lubna's hand an affectionate squeeze. "Our families have lived next door to each other in Jumeirah since before we were born, so we're practically related. Lubna's sister is even married to my older brother. They're both being primed to run a massive conglomerate one day, a merger of the Al Zarouni construction empire with the Al Nuaimi shipping empire. It's perfect, actually – lets the two of us off the hook to do what we want with our lives."

"Yes, and we've pledged to have fun together forever," a giggly Lubna interjected. "Amal's in the jewellery business and I'm an art dealer," she grandly proclaimed. "Specialising in nudes," she added, lowering her voice and giving me a wink.

"Is that legal in Dubai?" I replied. "I hear they even black out bum cracks and cleavage from *Vogue* and *Cosmo* before they're allowed into the country. How do you manage to trade in nude art?"

"Aha!" Lubna said, tapping her nose with her index finger and trying to look wise. "I have my ways."

Not very clever ways as it turned out three days later when I got a call from Amal.

"Hi sexy!"

"You've got the wrong number."

"I don't think so. *Chris Jones, Solicitor.* That's you, right? You gave me your card in the Buddha Bar the other night. Remember?"

"Oh yes, erm, Amal, isn't it?"

"That's right! And I have the perfect excuse to be calling you. We need a lawyer."

"*We* being...?"

"Lubna and me."

"How did I guess?"

"Because you're very clever. So clever, in fact, that you're going to be able to sort out our delicate little problem. Well, it's Lubna's little problem, to be precise."

"Doesn't Lubna's family have lawyers who can help her out? I work in-house for a company so I can't really get involved with private client work."

"Yes, but we can't go to them with this one. You are the perfect lawyer for the job and it will only take an hour of your time. We'll pick you up in twenty minutes, okay?"

"No, that's not okay," I replied, but I was speaking to myself.

Twenty minutes later, Priti on the front desk called through to let me know Amal Al Zarouni and Lubna Al Nuaimi were waiting for me in reception. I put on my jacket, grabbed my phone and headed down to the foyer, where I was hugged by Amal and propelled out through the revolving door by Lubna. A twenty-minute drive through town in a smart Range Rover brought us to a warehouse in Jebel Ali port where we were greeted by two customs officers and led inside towards a large wooden crate. Once we were all assembled in front of this crate, the younger of the two customs officers removed the front panel and tutted at the contents. When I took a look, I didn't think it was that bad, to be honest. Her breasts were covered with bits of seaweed and her nether regions were obscured by big blobs of sea foam, all very discreet really, but this young customs officer was having none of it. Lubna's statue of Aphrodite was 'obscene' and could not 'under any circumstances whatsoever' be permitted into the country.

"She's here for the Dubai Art Fair," Lubna whimpered, fluttering her eyelashes. "She's only staying for a week but they won't let her in."

"We need to find a creative solution," the older customs officer pronounced, sucking in his cheeks and pursing his rubbery lips. "So what do you think we can do?" The assembled group turned their attention to me, so I walked confidently toward the crate and read the shipping notice stuck to the side panel, playing for time really.

"Media City. That's in a free zone, isn't it?"

"Yes, it's part of TECOM."

"So, if Aphrodite were to go in a lorry straight to Media City from here, technically she wouldn't be landing onshore in Dubai, correct?"

"Yes! You are absolutely right!" the older customs officer enthusiastically replied. Unlike his younger counterpart, I'm sure he knew full well the country's obscenity laws apply equally in the free zones, but his appetite to find a workable solution for Little Miss *I'm So Important* Al Nuaimi was stronger than any need to educate his rookie colleague.

Suitably encouraged, I ventured on. "And if I were to sign a lawyer's undertaking that Aphrodite will go straight to her destination at Media City, stay for one week, and then leave the same way, we would have a solution, I think?"

"We would indeed," my co-conspirator replied with a smack of satisfaction.

So that's what we did. But that's not the end of the story, is it? Because guess what? Six weeks later I get a call late one evening from a certain young customs officer who's tidying his in-tray and can't find the export paperwork to marry up with a written undertaking I'd signed regarding a *'two metre statue of a famous marble woman from Greece with seaweed'*. It was a nerve-wracking few weeks that followed, I can tell you, whilst the authorities attempted to track down the absconding Aphrodite. I was expecting the proverbial knock at my door any minute, to be hauled away for questioning by the Dubai Legal Affairs Department followed by a striking off from the legal consultants' register, but Aphrodite was eventually tracked down to the private offices of a prominent Emirati minister and, given the circumstances, the paperwork got quickly filed away and no further action was taken.

But that doesn't mean I forgive Lubna for being responsible for the one professional undertaking I have ever breached. She made a fortune on that deal with the government minister, her one and only in the world of fine art, but she put my career on the line in the process. That woman's got a lot to answer for in many, many ways, yet watching her now, strolling through the garden arm-in-arm with Amal, butter wouldn't melt in that privileged little mouth of hers.

I'd like to be able to ignore them, to turn on my heels and go and tuck in to the food, but with less than two more weeks of this crap to put up with I wouldn't be doing myself any favours acting out of line this evening. So I hug Noura tight and steel myself for more of Fatima's usual gushing when it comes to this pair.

"Here you are at last! The party can really begin now you kids have arrived."

Kids? They're in their bloody forties.

"Where have you two jet-setters been this time?"

"Just Beirut for a quick twenty-four-hour visit. We're opening a new store there."

"Another one! How many are there now?"

"Oh mother, who's counting? It's going great, that's all you need to know." Amal gives Fatima a kiss on both cheeks. "Happy anniversary, by the way."

Credit where credit's due, the success of Just Jewels, Amal's retail business built on the concept of fair trade in the precious metals and gems industry, has been astounding. The industry and lifestyle are perfect, of course. Beautiful people, glamorous launch events, first-class air travel, glossy magazine interviews – you get the picture. There will still be elements of the 'rebel' child built into these trips as well: champagne at every reception, various flirtations and liaisons, nightclubs and casinos when the business day has ended, and fast cars to ride home in. Amal's family don't ask, as I'm sure they'd rather not know. I don't ask, simply because I'm not all that interested. I was once an element of Amal's rebel life, but since Noura and marriage came along, our relationship got too domesticated for Amal, who was quickly off in search of the next exciting adventure.

"We're opening in the Financial Centre, too," Amal now says, turning to me and scrutinizing my face for a reaction. "We've just signed a ten-year lease on the unit we saw there the other day. We're opening next month." And with that, Amal gives me a perfunctory peck on the cheek and takes Noura out of my arms.

Shit! We'll be running into each other constantly on that concourse.

But, hold on...my moment of panic is quickly swept away with a sudden realization. *Ha, I won't even be there.* Thank God! Imagine living constantly under the threat of exposure, going to work each morning and wondering whether today's the day you get busted and your colleagues find out you're a deceitful immoral bigamist.

"Congratulations! I'll look forward to seeing more of you then," I'm able to reply with genuine relish. "Maybe the occasional lunch date, if I'm lucky."

The puzzlement on Amal's face is priceless, but I don't get to enjoy the moment as much as I'd like because Noura's now pointing at the goat roasting on the spit and her bottom lip has started to wobble.

"Charlie!" she yells, "Charlie! Charlie! Charlie!" She tries to wriggle free from Amal's arms to make a dash for the fire pit.

"She thinks it's Barmy Charlie over there on the roasting spit," I try to explain, but Amal just looks at me blank. "You know," I add, "her favourite cartoon character? The hound dog that looks a bit like Snoopy?" But Amal just gives me the usual *'What the hell are you talking about now?'* glare before turning to Noura and snapping, "It's not a dog, it's a goat! Come on, I'll show you." And so Amal carries Noura wriggling and screaming over to the goat where a waiter is slicing meat off its hind leg and arranging it onto a platter. "See!" says Amal. "Not dog, is it?" Noura, momentarily silenced by the shock of seeing Charlie roasting up close, soon begins to re-erupt. *For god's sake, the poor child will be having nightmares for weeks now.* I'm heading over to Noura's aid when my way is blocked by a large man dressed in a grey pinstriped suit and purple paisley tie. "Don't I know you from somewhere?" he says, peering at me a little too closely.

"Erm, no, I don't think so," I say, trying to manoeuvre around him, but he's a persistent sod and won't be budged.

"The City perhaps? Do you work at Lloyd's by any chance?"

"Nope, I'm a lawyer actually, working between here and London."

Now Fatima has spotted Amal struggling with Noura and is gliding her way over to the fire pit to take control of the situation.

"Mmm, interesting." The guy's still scrutinising my face. "Any ties with Warwick Street Theatre, perhaps? Maybe that's where I've seen you?"

"Nope, that's not ringing any bells."

Fatima has now managed to get Amal and Noura sat down at a table and has pulled Noura onto her lap. She's picking up a piece of goat and is endeavouring to shovel some of the meat into Noura's mouth.

"I'm usually pretty good with faces. Well, I guess you must have a doppelgänger."

"Haha! That would be great, wouldn't it? Two of us to do the work."

Noura has now clocked the meat being force fed to her as cooked Charlie and is crying hysterically as only a toddler can.

"Please excuse me, I've got a small domestic situation to sort out over there."

As I reach the table, Fatima's wheedling, "It's just some meat," at Noura, whose screaming has now reached level ten, and Amal suddenly grabs the plate of goat from Fatima and flings it furiously across the table where it dumps its contents into the lap of Fatima's cousin, Zainab.

The other party guests at the table have now stopped their chatter and are watching us warily. One of them is picking a lump of greasy goat off the front of his otherwise crisp white kandoura. His wife's checking her hair for debris. I offer a general apology to everyone on Amal's behalf and turn to Fatima. "I could have told you Noura wouldn't eat goat!" I say, wrestling my daughter from her lap to try and calm her down.

"That girl watches too much bloody television!" This is Amal's helpful contribution to the mayhem. *Unbelievable!* 'That girl,' as Amal chooses to describe her, is our beautiful miracle child, the one who got born at twenty-three weeks, a whole week before the legal cut-off date for abortion, and survived, the one who's full of pluck and sparkle despite being the smallest kid in her class, the one we should be feeling incredibly thankful to have in our lives.

"Amal, will you just listen to yourself?" I snap. "She's going to cry and have tantrums every now and then, it's what three-year-olds do. You need to be the adult here and handle it."

"The way I see it," Fatima chimes in, "if her parents were around a bit more to do what parents are supposed to do, Noura would be a happy child and we wouldn't be having these family upsets all the time."

"Fatima, that's not really..."

"Urghhh, I can't handle this!" Amal snaps and jumps up, storming out through the garden gate so fast that Lubna has to put a bit of a trot on to catch up. And off they both go, leaving nothing but the odious cocktail of their expensive scents and a grumpy Fatima and Noura in their wake.

"I think it's time I took Noura home," I tell Fatima. "She's had enough."

And she's not the only one.

14.

Dubai

Noura's dead to the world by the time we get home, exhausted from the party, and I'm hoping I can get her changed and into bed without waking her up. The house is quiet, no sign of Amal (thank goodness), so I'm thinking a nice, relaxing glass of wine on the terrace before bedtime would be in order, but no sooner is the thought formed in my head and 'brrrr...brrrr...brrrr'; my bloody mobile's gone off. It's Mark and he knows it's late here, so it must be important, so I answer.

"Chris, hi! Sorry to bother you at this time of the evening but I need a minute of your time."

"No problem, Mark, I've just got home so your timing's good." *Blast! I've woken Noura up now.* There's the tell-tale sound of whimpering and she's starting to wriggle in my arms. "What can I do for you, Mark?" I say, jigging Noura up and down on my hip and trying to shush her back to sleep.

"The chaps in your London office inform me they're ready to exchange contracts on the casino land deal," Mark tells me, "but before I give them the green light I need your reassurance the Bailey's Dubai deal is going to close at the end of next week. As you know, we'll be rolling the proceeds from the sale straight into the casino development and I don't want to be caught short."

Erm, no I didn't know that, actually. I thought my little chat with Grace the other day had put an end to Mark's great plans of bringing Las Vegas to Broadstairs.

"Wow, that was fast work. I thought it'd be several weeks before the searches and enquiries on that transaction would be complete?" I say to Mark.

Noura's not settling, so I make my way down the hall and knock on my maid's door. "Sorry, Rose," I mouth when she answers and I hand Noura to her.

"Turns out your guys acted for the previous buyers, who had to pull out because they lost their funding," Mark says. "All the due diligence was pretty much already done."

Mark is starting to read out bits of the due diligence report to me, a potentially lengthy process I realise, so I make my way into the kitchen, pour myself a glass of wine from the fridge, a delicious Chablis I'd opened yesterday, and go out onto the terrace. The night is warm and sultry – misty glass weather – and when I sit down I feel the captured heat from the daytime radiating from the deck and warming my legs. The compound's all quiet apart from a couple of teenagers at the far end of the swimming pool, dangling their feet in the water and chatting quietly. I love this place, these twelve single-storey villas set around a shared recreation area, built thirty years ago for expat families and now my time-worn little oasis. Amal hates it, of course, and has been hoping for the long-anticipated demolition order to come through the door at any time, requiring us to vacate to make room for yet another new and swanky master-planned neighbourhood.

"...and last but not least," Mark's saying, with far more energy than I can hope to match, "even though it's ex-Church land, the title's clear of any restrictive covenants that could prevent commercial development."

"That's all well and good," I say, "but the previous buyers wanted the land for a retail park, didn't they? An entertainment venue, especially one incorporating a casino, is a totally different ballgame. First of all, you need to find someone with an existing casino license in the Thanet area who's willing to sell it to you, then you need the permission of the Gambling Commission to buy it, and then you need to apply to the local council to move the license to your site. At that point, there might be objections from the police or members of the public, then who knows what will happen after that. Are you sure you'll be able to jump through all those hoops, or have you become a gambling man already?"

"C'mon, Chris, luck is on our side with this one – I can feel it in my bones."

"And are your bones also telling you the Bailey's Dubai sale will close without any snags? Because you know a deal's not done until it's done. All you've got so far with Al Shamsi is a non-binding preliminary contract. It could still abort if he decides to start messing around."

A sudden whoosh-and-hiss from next door's patch of garden triggers a cat to come flying over the partition and land on the table right in front of me, making me jump and grab for my glass, but it's just the neighbour's irrigation system turning on and the cat hops down and slinks away into the night.

"Don't go getting wobbly on me, Chris. Let's get the Dubai deal done and then you can get your arse back over here to kick-start the casino development work. Everything's on track in Dubai, I believe?"

"So far, yes, but..."

I can see the skyscrapers of Sheikh Zayed Road from here, silhouetted like the jagged printout from a lie detector test. *God, I wonder what mine would look like if I took one now?*

"Great! That's all I need to hear," says Mark. "We'll speak again soon, Chris. Have a good evening."

"Yep, I'll be sure to do that."

I disconnect my call with Mark and make my way to Noura's room to check she's settled down okay. Rose is just coming out when I get there, slowly closing the door behind her. "She's sleeping," she whispers. "We had to find Barmy Charlie first, but once she had him to cuddle she quickly dropped off."

"Thanks, Rose, you're a star." It had taken me a while to warm to the idea of having a maid around, a stranger sharing your living space and witnessing the ins and outs of your family's life, but I have to admit Amal was right to insist on us hiring Rose back when Noura was born and our little instant family had first been flung together. Rose has been like the wife neither of us had, filling the domestic void perfectly. She'd been an easy hire, too, coming highly recommended by Lubna's family, the Al Nuaimis, who'd had Rose's cousin Analyn working for them for several years. I still get uncomfortable at the thought of the tittle-tattle that must go on between those two about their respective employers, but we wouldn't entertain Rose sharing Al Nuaimi household gossip with us and the Al Nuaimis have said they take the same line with Analyn.

"Get yourself off to bed now," I tell Rose, making my way back out to the garden. I need to call Grace. I try her home number and she picks up on the second ring. *Yep, she's probably sat waiting for Mark to get home for his dinner.*

"Grace, it's Chris."

"Oh, hi Chris. Mark's not here actually, he's still at the office."

"I know, I've just spoken to him. Actually, it's you I'm after."

"Twice in two weeks? Should I be worried?" she says with a nervous chuckle.

She must think I'm a walking bag of problems with everything I've brought to her over the years. It's a wonder she still picks up the phone to me, but she always does. She may be the wife of my most important client, but she's also become the mother I wish I'd had. I remember years ago Alex and I were around their place for a cocktail party one time, celebrating the launch of another of Mark's apartment developments perhaps, I can't really remember, and I'd received an email from my actual mother half way through the evening. After years of silence it had been a real bolt out of the blue, waffling on about grandchildren being a chance to rectify parental mistakes or some such crap, and could she please meet Josh, spend some time with him. Grace had found me in the kitchen and asked if I was okay and I'd ended up telling her the whole sordid story of my family when I was growing up, and she had given me the strength to say 'no' to my mother's request, to trust that letting her into Josh's life wouldn't be the best thing to do.

"I know we spoke about this last week," I tell Grace now, "but I thought you should know the latest," and I fill her in on my conversation with Mark. "He's supposed to be taking his foot off the accelerator to look after his health," I finish, "but with the pressure of trying to pull off these two deals back-to-back with no certainty over either of them, that's definitely not happening."

"Thanks, Chris. I agree, it is a worry. I wish he'd get out of that damn casino project, but you know what he's like. Look, leave it with me. I'll try speaking with him again."

"Thanks, Grace, and good luck," I say, disconnecting.

There's one more call to make before I turn in, and that's to Tom to get his take on the events of my evening. I go into the kitchen to top up my glass and to check there's no spouse or maid lurking around – I need privacy for this one. I go back outside and settle into my chair. The two teenagers have left the poolside by now and next door's irrigation has stopped its hissing. The silence is even more total than earlier, encouraging my nerves to shift into a lower gear.

"Mark will come round once he knows the full facts," Tom says after I've filled him in. "And as for everyone else – Fatima, Amal, Lubna, *et cetera* – they're irrelevant, aren't they? Keep focused on the plan, Chris. That's all you need to do."

My call with Tom is reassuring, it always is, and I'm just gathering myself up to go inside when I hear the unmistakable slap of flip-flops on tiles, making their swift exit out of the kitchen and down the hall. *Rose! How much has she overheard? This is exactly why I don't like having a maid in the home.*

15.

Dubai
Nine days to Closing

It's ten o'clock on Tuesday morning so I'm at Marwan Al Shamsi's office for our meeting. Except he isn't here. "He's five minutes away," I'm told by the sulky local sat behind the reception desk. Fact or guesstimate I'm not sure, but I decide not to provoke the receptionist's disdain by questioning this further. She's fluttering her eyelashes at me now, but this isn't misdirected flattery, you understand – she's just trying to keep her eyes open under the sheer mass of her extensions. "Take a seat over there and wait," she says, waving me toward the waiting area. I take a seat as directed and watch as she picks up the phone. "Romeo, come!" she snaps into the receiver, then drops it back in its cradle and returns to what are presumably her default activities of shuffling papers and pout-practising with her over-filled plum-glossed lips. I bet she's dressed from head to toe in skin-tight designer gear under that black abaya and shayla, another Kardashian localisation project.

A few minutes go by (which I spend reflecting on the contradictions of Emirati culture and glancing pointedly at the wall clock every so often) and the duly summoned

Romeo comes trotting into reception. He's the office boy from the all-night meeting three weeks back and he breaks into a toothy grin when he sees me. "Hello again," he says, jigging from foot to foot. "Please, this way. I'll take you to your office and you can wait for Mr Al Shamsi there."

If you met Romeo you'd think he was about eleven years old. He's no more than five feet and looks ready for school in his work-supplied navy trousers and candy-striped shirt, but I know from our previous chats he's actually thirty-three and has a wife and two kids back at home in the Philippines. He's hoping to work himself up to a sufficient grade to sponsor them to come and live here...*hold on, did he just say 'your' office?*

"I don't think so, Romeo," I say, shaking my head.

"Oh! You want to wait here instead?"

"No. I mean, it's not *my* office."

"It's not?"

"No, of course it's not."

"Sorry, I must have misunderstood."

"No worries, Romeo." *He's going to have to pull his socks up if he wants that promotion.* "Lead the way," I say, smiling my sympathies as I get to my feet.

Romeo leads me down a well-lit, broad corridor and into a corner office suite which, wow, I wish actually *was* my office. Floor-to-ceiling windows on two sides look out over the Creek toward new Dubai, the glinting water serving as an alluring backdrop for the myriad of workday stories being acted out every which way you look. A businessman hails a taxi that turns on its hazard lights and swerves to the kerbside to pick him up; an abra driver docks at a berth, aided by a colleague on the jetty who catches his rope; three fishermen on a trawler untangle their nets whilst another shoos away seagulls as he mops the deck; a coconut water vendor pulls his cart along the quayside toward a group of schoolchildren huddled around a teacher who's filling their minds with Dubai history. I take a seat on the guest sofa – a beautiful blush-coloured nubuck leather two-seater, perfect for sinking into for a bit of people-watching – and allow myself to be soothed by the muted hum of office life from beyond the door that Romeo has left slightly ajar. Why have I been called here today? And to meet with the big guy himself? I could have done with getting a better night's sleep, to be honest, to deal with whatever Al Shamsi's got to throw at me, but with the events of the evening still buzzing around my head it took me forever to drop off, and when I eventually did I was thrown into the most bizarre dream I can ever remember having.

We were on a plane flying somewhere. I'm not sure where to, but we were all there. Yes, all of us. I was in Business with the two kids. Amal and Lubna were up in First, and Alex and James were somewhere back in Economy. When I looked out the airplane window it was onto a cartoon world and I could see Barmy Charlie at the window of a blue plastic plane flying alongside us. He was waving to a life-sized toy goat on wheels that was flying past upside down. Somehow I knew Tom was up front piloting the plane and I shouted down the aisle to tell him he didn't know how to fly, but he couldn't hear me up in the cockpit and I couldn't find my phone to call him. I knew I had to get up there to help him, but I was buckled into my seat and I couldn't get out and then we were nose-diving toward the ground, and the kids, who weren't wearing seatbelts, slid off their seats and disappeared under the row in front of them, and we were plummeting, faster, faster...

"So what do you think?" Al Shamsi is suddenly present, oblivious to my mental meanderings and sweeping his arm broadly across the room.

"About what?" I say, quickly tapping my phone and turning it face-down.

"The office, of course! Is it grand enough for you? Do you like the décor?"

"Erm... yes... it's very nice..."

"It would need a bit of personalising, of course – a few photos of the family, or perhaps it would be *families* in your case?" he says, raising his eyebrows with a mischievousness I wouldn't have expected from him.

Okay, so Al Shamsi's in the know about my situation, Haddad has squealed.

"Perhaps a rug or two. But that would be up to you, of course."

This should be interesting, if he's hinting at what I think he is...

"I'm not entirely sure I follow."

"Well, Haddad tells me... Ah, there you are!" Al Shamsi's attention is abruptly diverted by Romeo, who has entered the room carrying a tray of water and dates.

"We'll take coffee as well, please, Romeo," says Al Shamsi, settling himself behind the expansive partners desk that has potential to be mine and shifting his bum around in the leather seat to get nice and comfy. "How do you take your coffee, Chris?" He's fidgeting with the knobs and levers under the chair now, getting it set up just right.

"Black, no sugar is fine thanks," I reply.

"Two black coffees then," Al Shamsi tells Romeo.

"With milk, sir?" The look on Romeo's face is so earnest it hurts; he's desperate to make a positive impression with his big boss, but all it earns him from Al Shamsi is a stony look. It's not such a dumb question, though: I know where he's coming from.

"Good question, Romeo!" I say. "The last time I asked for white coffee in Dubai, I got a cup of hot rosewater. It's a Lebanese thing, isn't it? I'll have a black coffee, no milk, please."

"Two black coffees, no milk!" Al Shamsi snaps impatiently. "And fetch it from the coffee shop downstairs, none of that dishwater soup you make."

"Yes sir, no sir," replies Romeo, retreating backwards out of the room.

"HR tell me he's after a promotion to a desk job," says Al Shamsi, watching the door closing. "You wouldn't believe it," he continues, turning his attention to me, "there's five different coffee machines in this office – filter, espresso, capsules, fully automatic, semi-automatic – and he's incapable of producing a decent cup of coffee from any of them."

"Oh dear," I say.

"But perhaps you will soon find that out for yourself."

"Right..."

Al Shamsi has obviously called me here this morning to offer me a job, but the question is, why? Extra incentive to ensure I don't find those 'lost' due diligence documents? But surely Al Shamsi wouldn't get his own hands dirty with this, implicate himself in blackmail, bribery, fraud – that's what he's got Haddad for.

"Haddad tells me you're married into the Al Zarouni family," Al Shamsi continues, evoking the slimeball right on cue. "To Amal Al Zarouni?"

"That's right, but it's not something I generally talk about. I find it's better to keep your private life private."

"I bet you do!" says Al Shamsi with a smirk. "But the Emirati community is a small one, Chris. Tight like this," he continues, clasping his hands together to emphasise his point. "There are very few secrets amongst us. We all know what's going on with each other. For example, just last Friday after prayers I was sat in your father-in-law's maglis along with a few others, catching up on the week's news. Abdullah was telling us about a neighbour of ours who'd conducted himself badly in a business matter. Omar Bin Fahad...?" Al Shamsi pauses to see if I recognise the name, but it's not familiar to me so I shrug and he continues. "He was the sponsor of an Australian gentleman who died in a cycling accident a few months ago, knocked off his bike by a drunk behind the wheel of a Ferrari in the early hours of one Saturday morning. Omar owned fifty-one percent of the Australian guy's company on paper, a classic sponsorship arrangement where the Emirati gets paid an annual fee for legally holding fifty-one percent of the shares in the company beneficially for the foreigner, the true owner of the company. Only in this case, the usual side agreements acknowledging the Ozzie guy's full ownership of the company weren't in place and Omar claimed he owned fifty-one percent outright, that his contribution to the capital that earned him the fifty-one percent had been 'in kind' – networking and bringing in business, calling in debts, that sort of thing – and that his annual sponsorship payments were actually toward his share of profits.

"When the company was sold by the dead man's widow, Omar took seventy percent of the net sale proceeds as his own: fifty-one percent plus a further nineteen for his 'undrawn profit'. The poor widow had to reach a swift out-of-court settlement with Omar before she was forced to leave the country with the kids when her residence visa got cancelled. It was all supposed to be confidential, but there's no such thing in our community. Omar has blotted his card now; nobody's going to trust him again in quite the same way. On the other hand, the Al Zarounis, now they're a different case, they're very well respected. There's been nothing to tarnish their reputation. Not yet, anyway."

This is beginning to sound like blackmail.

"Can I ask why you've brought me here today, Mr Al Shamsi?"

Al Shamsi's face is impassive, inscrutable. I prefer a frown or a glare – you know where you are with those – but an impassive face? That's a shield for thoughts far darker than you can hope to fathom or wish to know.

"Sorry I'm late." Haddad comes slithering into the room at this point, says good morning to us both and takes a seat on the sofa next to me.

"Haddad, good of you to join us," says Al Shamsi. "I've just been telling Chris about the power of local gossip."

"Ah yes, the all-knowing Emirati grapevine," says Haddad, nodding gravely and trying to look wise.

"Indeed. It's the fabric of our community," says Al Shamsi. "It lets us know who we should bring into our inner circle and who we should block. But quite right," he says, glancing at his watch, "we're not here to gossip. Let me get to the point of the meeting."

Finally!

"Ah, here's the coffee at last!" Romeo's back, and the three of us watch in silence as he serves coffees with chocolates to

Al Shamsi and me, a glass of water to Haddad, and reverses his way out the door, closing it softly behind him.

"Haddad tells me you might be looking for a new job when your role with Mark Bailey finishes?" says Al Shamsi. "Something that takes you back and forth between here and London."

Here we go...

"Yes, but the chances of that happening are very slim," I reply. Al Shamsi sinks deeper into his chair and narrows his eyes. "I was hoping my firm would open an office here and I could be a part of that, but that's not going to happen in the foreseeable future," I continue as he begins inspecting his fingernails. "So it looks like I'm back to London full-time from the end of the month," I conclude.

"Haddad tells me your knowledge of the law here in Dubai is quite impressive, that the contract you prepared for the Bailey's Dubai deal is technically very solid. How did you learn all of that?"

"Well, compared with other jurisdictions like the UK, the legal system here is relatively easy to grasp," I reply. "As soon as I arrived here, I read all the main Federal and Dubai laws – the English translations of them, anyway – and since then I've had a lot of help from a friend of mine who works over at Al Hattan & Co. He's helped me to get to grips with the practical implementation of the various laws because, as you know, that can diverge quite substantially from the written word."

Al Shamsi's phone rings before he's got chance to comment on this. He checks who's calling, smiles and connects his earpiece.

"Yes habibti, of course...no problem...Mahmoud is going to drive you there...mmm, four o'clock...and then he will collect you afterwards...yes, at seven...eleven, is she? And you've got a present to take with you?"

I surmise this is his daughter he's talking too, and he's in no rush to finish his call. Meanwhile, Haddad and I are sat on the sofa like lemons.

"Mafi mushkila habibiti, khallas. *No problem my dear, it's done.* I will see you at home later."

"My daughter," says Al Shamsi, putting the phone down and looking at Haddad and me with an expression of indulgence on his face that I realise we're supposed to warmly acknowledge somehow. Bollocks to that! Can you imagine the reaction in the room if I'd been the one taking a call from my daughter?

"Shall we move on?" I say. "There's things I need to attend to back at the office."

Al Shamsi removes the black hoop and white cotton ghutra from his head, ruffles then smooths his (surprisingly short and tufty) hair, puts the scarf and hoop back on his head and fusses it all back into place before reaching for his coffee.

"Always direct, Chris. I like that. So I will be direct with you. I'd like to offer you a position here at Shamal Enterprises. Once we've closed our acquisition of Bailey's Dubai, we'd like you to come over to us as our head of legal." He's admiring his fingernails again, I see. They've certainly had a buffing at the grooming salon recently judging from their sheen – probably this morning whilst I was sat waiting for him in reception – and he seems pretty taken with the result. "I'm very impressed with what I've seen of your work so far, Chris, and with our London business portfolio expanding and your historical knowledge of Bailey's Dubai, I'm sure you'd quickly become a valuable asset to us. You get to keep your London-Dubai lifestyle going and we get ourselves a new in-house lawyer."

It's still not absolutely clear whether Haddad is working alone in his little scheme to knock ten million dollars off the Bailey's Dubai sale price or, as I suspect, Al Shamsi's the great mastermind here, pulling Haddad's strings from above? I need to know one way or the other, and the moment of truth has arrived.

"So you're confident the deal will close, then?" I venture. "We've still got some outstanding due diligence requirements to fulfil from Mark's side."

"Yes, and I understand from Haddad you're assisting us with that. Look, I actually believe the company is worth forty million, not the fifty million Mark Bailey is asking for, but we need a negotiating tool and that's where you come in. I'm leaving the mechanics of that up to you and Haddad to work out, but get me that ten million reduction, and as far as I'm concerned you're part of my team."

Gotcha!

"I'll be in touch," says Al Shamsi abruptly, getting to his feet. He comes across to Haddad and me, shakes my hand, dazzles us both with his Hollywood smile and swooshes out of the room.

My interview is over.

16.

London
Seven days to Closing

Amal and Lubna are lovers, right? Okay, I get they're lifelong neighbours, business partners, kindred souls even, but there's an added ingredient to their relationship keeping them glued to each other's side and I've been sure for a while now they're more than just good friends. What other explanation can there be? Well, I had lunch with Amal's father today and he had quite a different take on the whole Amal/Lubna dynamic, which he chose to share with me at the tail end of a bottle of red wine (most of which had been drunk by him, I might add). We'd been chatting about the usual stuff when we meet up in London – real estate hot spots, international trade wars, escalating political dramas in the Middle East, that sort of thing – certainly no family stuff, we just don't have that kind of relationship. Imagine my surprise, then, when out of the blue he asked, "How are you and Amal getting along?" and he was suddenly staring at me, expecting a response.

"Erm..." I glanced at my phone and willed it to ring, to provide me with the excuse I needed to bring our lunch to a hasty close and rush back to the office.

"I've wanted to talk to you since the party the other night," Abdullah continued. "Amal shouldn't have stormed off with Lubna like that and I can understand why you might be upset."

This sounded like a trick question to me. I decided to admire the view out of the restaurant window. *Great location*, I thought. *There's the Millennium Bridge over there, and that's St Paul's I can see, just across the Thames...*

"You know, Chris, I haven't told you this before, but you have a very important place in the Al Zarouni family."

...Lovely sunny day, as well. We could almost be in Dubai except Abdullah isn't wearing his kandoura and he seems to have drunk too much wine.

"I know you felt pressured into marrying Amal when Noura was born, and we were all thrown together by circumstances, one could say, but you're a good person, and a very positive influence on Amal."

...I've never heard Abdullah speak like this.

"I mean it, Amal has really settled down in the last three years, and we have you to thank for that."

...He must be after something.

"It hasn't always been the case, but honestly speaking, we're very proud of Amal now."

...Eh? Proud? Surely he thinks the same as everyone else, that Amal's a spoilt brat whose behaviour is a constant source of embarrassment to the entire Al Zarouni family?

"Just Jewels is a remarkable success," he continued. "Twenty-six stores in nine countries throughout the Middle East and growing fast. It's really quite an achievement."

"Well, yes, I can see where you're coming from," I replied, relieved to hear the conversation return to safe ground. "We haven't seen much of the profit yet since it's all been ploughed back in to fund the regional expansion. But the company didn't get built by itself and I suppose it's worth a decent sum on paper."

"Indeed, and all this as well as handling the ongoing situation with Lubna."

"I'm not sure I catch your drift?"

"No, I didn't think you would," Abdullah replied. He then paused, taking a sip of water before glancing at me and quickly away again, letting his focus settle on the middle distance. He seemed hesitant, now that he'd brought the conversation to this point. "Okay," he said finally, placing his hands firmly on the table. "I'm going to tell you a story. To be frank, it's one we'd all rather forget, but it's important now for you to hear it. Then you will understand why Amal is so wrapped up with Lubna much of the time and your concerns will be finally laid to rest."

I glanced at my watch, mindful of my two-thirty video call with Dimple back at the office. "I haven't got long, Abdullah, you'll have to keep it short, I'm afraid."

"Five minutes," he replied. "It will be worth it, I can assure you."

...I really don't need this.

"I'm all ears, Abdullah. Please go on."

Abdullah filled his glass with water and hastily gulped some down before proceeding. "Amal was at school with Lubna's brother, Jaber," he began.

...Lubna's got a brother?

"And when they were twelve years old," he continued, "they'd both gone on a school camping trip to Wadi Madbah. It's a natural beauty spot in the mountains just over the border with Oman and is full of waterfalls and rock pools. You might have heard of it? Or even flown over it at

AMBIGAMIST 125

some stage?" I nodded, keen to push him on to the end of the story and make a swift exit. "The group had set up camp for the night on a ledge above one of the pools. Despite a forecast for clear weather, it began to pour with rain in the early hours of the morning. Amal decided to go for a swim in the pool, which was quickly filling up with rainwater fed from the torrent gushing down the mountainside. It seems that Amal got swept away by the force of the water to the far side of the pool and was in danger of being driven over the edge and down into the ravine. Jaber was a strong swimmer and jumped in to rescue Amal. Tragically, though, Jaber had also underestimated the strength of the torrent and *he* was the one that got swept over the edge. He plummeted fifty feet to his death on the rocks below. Everyone blamed Amal for the accident, of course. As you can imagine, it was a very dark time for all of us. But that's not the point of the story." Abdullah glanced at me at this stage, checking he had my full attention. "The point is, Lubna was devastated by the loss of her brother and, in turn, Amal was wracked with guilt and pledged to make amends. And here we are thirty years later and Amal is still trying to make amends."

It's 'why Amal took Lubna into the business and made her a partner'. It's 'why they're practically inseparable'. It's 'why things are the way they are'. According to Abdullah, at least.

According to me, it's total bullshit.

And according to Abdullah, there's nothing for me to be worried about when it comes to Amal's relationship with Lubna because Amal loves me and Noura very much, blah, blah, blah.

Also bullshit.

I know Amal pretty well, better than Abdullah does, that's for sure, and no way is it atoning for Jaber's death, thirty-year-old guilt or any other such laudable nonsense that's keeping Amal glued to Lubna's side. Abdullah's one of those men who expects to be believed no matter what crap they come out with, and this is just his brash attempt at keeping me placated on the matrimonial front. He certainly has a vested interest in trying to keep my marriage to Amal together, to bring the sheen of respectability and some stability to Amal's life, not to mention holding Noura, their one and only grandchild, in the bosom of the Al Zarouni family and keeping Fatima content. But I'm afraid Abdullah's little intervention is not going to succeed. I know what decades worth of guilt looks like, I've explored it thoroughly with the considerable help of Ms Belinda Potts PGDip, BACP, and it's nothing like this.

"Let's talk about your childhood," Belinda had said during my third session with her.

"Let's not," I'd replied. "I don't really believe in looking back."

"Interesting," said Belinda. "Do you want to tell me more about that?"

"No, not really."

"Let's start with your student days. I think you told me you were at Uni in London?"

"Yes."

"Why don't you tell me about that?" she'd suggested.

So I told her I'd kept a journal when I was at Uni and she could read that if she was interested. She told me she was very interested, that I should bring it to our next session and that I should read it to myself in the meantime. So I read it, every word of it. And then I needed more than one counselling session to get over it. I've still got the journal, it's locked up in my desk at work and I get it out every so often when I need the reminder. The important entries are flagged with Post-it notes, once bright yellow but now a grubby mustard colour. Read them and judge me:

Sunday 20th September, 1998

Hello Journal!

My first day of University has finally arrived!!

Freedom at last!!!

Ten minutes out of Bristol and I already feel my future pulling me along the train tracks straight toward London and beyond.

I'm putting home well and truly behind me now. If Mum or Ryan want to get hold of me, they know where I am.

As today is the first day of the rest of my life, I thought it would be fitting to spend some time thinking about everything I want to achieve in life – because if you can imagine it, you can achieve it.

So here goes:

1. Get a degree and qualify as a lawyer.
2. Train as a professional photographer in parallel – my Plan B, just in case.

3. Work for UNICEF or similar humanitarian organization – do some good in the world.
4. Settle down, get married, have kids – sounds easy enough, but a difficult one to get right.
5. Travel the world.
6. Learn to fly.

That would be a life well-lived.

I can't wait to get started!!!

*

Monday 5th October, 1998

Wow, wow wow!!!

I went to a Sociology of Law lecture this morning and it has really got me thinking. I'd never questioned it before, but take an issue such as getting into debt. It's not a crime, it's a civil court matter between a creditor and debtor, right? Well, it turns out it depends where you live, because in some countries getting into debt is a crime and a debtor will go to jail.

Law is a product of everything else that makes up a place – its religion, politics, social pressures, economics, culture. Issues such as abortion, theft, inheritance, debt, bigamy, can all be treated differently depending upon which country you're in.

Much of what I consider to be wrong isn't wrong everywhere, and much of what I consider to be right isn't right everywhere.

Question: If there's no universal agreement on something, is it okay to do the 'wrong' thing for the 'right' reasons?

Answer: Perhaps in that situation it comes down to a person's individual (instinctive?) moral judgment???

My mind has been opened today!

*

Friday 27th November, 1998

It's still all quiet on the home front. No news is good news as far as that's concerned.

Grape picking in Italy next Summer??? I can earn some money, meet new people and see a different country all at the same time. Why not?

Here are my Top 5 countries I want to visit:

1. South Africa – Nelson Mandela's Long Walk to Freedom is still the most inspirational book I've ever read.
2. India – home to another complete legend of a lawyer-turned-activist, Mahatma Gandhi.
3. USA – but it's such a vast country, where to begin?

4. Saudi Arabia – just because I've heard so much controversial stuff about this country, I want to see it for myself. Is it really illegal for women to drive there, or for couples to hold hands in public???
5. Israel/Palestine – to see this 100-year old conflict with my own eyes and try to make sense of it.

Anyway, Italy next Summer would be a good place to start.

*

Thursday 14th January, 1999

Major news of the day: I've reached the conclusion that I'm a liberal.

Liberals support civil rights, democracy, secularism, gender equality, racial equality, freedom of speech, freedom of religion and press freedom.

That's me in a nutshell, I just didn't have a word for it before.

Evidence:

1. Gender equality is a no-brainer. Male chambermaids, female astronauts...Bring it on!
2. I believe in abortion. What if Mum hadn't terminated her last pregnancy? It would have been a complete disaster.

3. Most religions seem to agree on life's important rules, e.g. don't kill, don't steal, don't lie, so why does it really matter what religion you are? Provided you're a good person and observe these rules, as far as I'm concerned you can belong to any religion you want, or none at all.
4. As far as I'm aware I don't know any gay people, but I'm totally fine with the idea of it.
5. If I could swap places with Nelson Mandela when he was my age, I would. He's such an icon of equality and freedom.

Good to know.

*

Thursday 18th March, 1999

A shocking thought from today's Family Law lecture.

The Children Act 1989 – responsible parents have the following duties towards their children:
·   provide a home for the child
·   protect and maintain the child
·   discipline the child
·   choose and provide for the child's education
·   agree to the child's medical treatment
·   name the child and agree to any change of name
·   look after the child's property

Surely, of all the laws out there, this is the most important one of all? To care for and protect children.

Mum has been breaking this law since the day it was enacted.

*

Monday 24th May, 1999

Bad news today.

I got a letter from Mum and now I'm going to have to cancel my Italy trip this Summer.

Apparently I'm selfish, I only ever think of myself, why would I want a career in the law anyway when there's perfectly good jobs I could already be doing in Bristol, why can't I be like other kids on the estate, nothing's ever good enough for me, I've turned my back on my family, Ryan's missing me, I've let her down, I hate hard work so how am I going to manage to pick grapes all Summer, I should be at home to support her, her, her...

In short, I'm back to bloody Bristol for the Summer.

Okay, enough of that for now, I've got stacks of work to get through this afternoon. More of the dreaded journal later, and you'll see what I mean when I tell you: if anyone is living with the daily burden of old guilt, it's not bloody Amal.

17.

London

I am trying to put my lunchtime bullying session with Abdullah behind me and am on my video call with Dimple. It's going on a bit and I'm squirming in my seat about the 'lost' documents she's still scrambling to find.

"But Chris, are you sure they're not in one of those boxes we brought from store last week?" she says.

"No, they were the early drafts. We need the final signed originals."

"I know, Chris, but..."

"I can only suggest you keep looking. Search through everything again. They're there somewhere."

"I'm doing my best, Chris, but they're simply not here. Let's raise this with Mark. Maybe he can think of a solution?"

Blast! My mobile's ringing now. I dig it out of my bag and see it's Josh calling from his new phone.

"Leave me to speak with Mark. You just keep looking," I tell Dimple, tapping my mouse and putting her and the problem of lost documents out of sight and mind for now.

"There's a man at the front door and I'm here on my own," Josh says when I pick up. "I don't know if I should answer or just wait for him to go away?" He's speaking quietly, almost in a whisper, but I can hear the tremble in his voice and my gut wrenches.

This is all too much for a nine-year-old, isn't it? First the intruder incident, then being left overnight at the theatre. It's no wonder he's scared.

He tells me Alex 'went out for cigarettes' over an hour ago and hasn't got back yet. I tell him not to answer the door and to stay put in his room with Margo: I'm on my way home and will be there in twenty minutes.

Five minutes later, as I'm getting into a cab outside my office building, my phone rings again.

"He's still there, and he's banging the door really hard now."

"Just stay in your room with Margo," I repeat. "I'll be there soon, okay?"

I hang up, take one look at the snarled-up traffic ahead and dial 999. I'm getting jittery too, now, what with everything that's going on. Haddad? James *bloody* O'Leary? It could even be Alex's frigging hash dealer at the door, for all I know. I'm taking no chances. I give the operator my address and ask for a police car to go there urgently.

I call Alex and get voicemail.

By the time I reach home, the front door is wide open and a policeman is stood on the doorstep talking into his radio. He looks just like Good Cop from my nightmare, the one with the nice smiley face.

Shit, he's not smiling. My door's been kicked in! My dark angel is here in my head again, telling me I've lost Josh, that I've failed him. I rush into the house, yelling to Good Cop, "Where is he? Where is he?" as I go. "In the kitchen," the policeman shouts after me. *The kitchen! Thank God! He's here.* I dash along the hallway and into the kitchen. There's Margo, sat beside the table. And there's Josh, right by her side. He's talking to a policewoman. *Crap, it's Bad Cop.* Built like a bull and looking as snarky as a seasoned film critic.

Josh is shifting his bum around nervously in his seat as he's telling Bad Cop, "But I'm not left on my own *all* that often," and that pervasive sick feeling is back with me, filling me up inside.

I tell Bad Cop I'm a lawyer and was unavoidably held up at work, that I was supposed to be home three hours ago, but I had a client emergency to deal with, blah, blah, blah, and eventually they leave, with Good Cop giving us a cheery wave and Bad Cop threatening to 'be back' if anything 'looking like child neglect' should ever be reported for our address again.

Now that they're gone, Josh fills me in on his full conversation with Bad Cop, about how she was asking all kinds of questions concerning his mum and dad: who is usually at home to look after him, how often is he left home alone and that sort of thing. This can't go on, can it? Alex's behaviour has only become more reckless since I quit feigning ignorance about the affair with James *bloody* O'Leary. Who still hasn't given his front door key back, by the way.

By the time Alex gets home several hours later Josh is up in his room with Margo. I can hear him laughing, probably at something he's watching on TV, and it's good to hear my boy back in good spirits after his ordeal this afternoon. Seems Alex is in good spirits too, judging from the caterwauling

I can hear advancing unsteadily down the hall and into the kitchen. *I am what I am...* Fridge opening. Clink, clink. Fridge slamming closed. Cupboard opening. Glass down on counter. Cupboard slamming. Glug, glug, glug into the glass. *Till you can shout out...* Caterwauling stops for swig of wine. Caterwauling resumes. *I am what I am...* All without a care in the world.

"Where the hell have you been all day?" I blast, bursting into the kitchen.

"Darling! You're home."

"We've had the bloody police here today because Josh was left home alone. It will be the social services on our doorstep next," I shout, "and I wouldn't blame them! You're so loved up with James *bloody* O'Leary, and off your head on booze and pot the whole time, you can't even remember you've got a nine-year-old son to look after!"

The doorbell rings. What now! Still breathless from ranting, I go to answer it and find Jim Green from next door standing there bearing a padded envelope.

"No one answered your door when the courier guy came earlier, so he dropped this round to me," he explains. "I tried knocking myself, but there was nobody at home."

The package is addressed to Chris Jones, and the shipper is Mr S Haddad, Shamal Enterprises, Dubai. Why the hell is Haddad sending stuff to my London home address? I stash the envelope in my briefcase in the hall and go back into the kitchen where Alex has had time to think about what I've said.

"If you're such a fantastic parent, you stay at home and look after him!" And with that helpful response Alex stumbles down the hall and back out the front door, giving it a superior slam for good measure.

Fucking brilliant!

I go and retrieve the courier package from my briefcase and take it into the kitchen. At least I now know it was just the courier guy and our neighbour knocking on the front door this afternoon. Alex's wine glass is still on the counter so I top it up from the bottle and take a good long glug. I slit the envelope open and pull out the contents: a photograph and a letter. I flip the photo over and see 'Happy Families No. 2' scrawled across the back. I put the photo on the table in disgust and start to read the letter.

Dear Chris,

Thank you for meeting with our Chairman, Mr Marwan Al Shamsi, earlier this week to discuss the Head of Legal position available at Shamal Enterprises. Accordingly, we are setting out below the...

"Who's that?"

God! I nearly jump out of my skin. Josh is stood beside me, studying the photo with an odd look of curiosity. And not without good reason. It's a photo of me holding Noura, taken last week at the beach park where we'd gone to fly her new kite.

"It's the daughter of a friend of mine over in Dubai," I say, aware that I'm lying to my son, whom I promised just last week I'd never lie to, but focused nonetheless on scanning the letter to get its overall gist...*terms of offer...* *conditional on the successful closing of...reporting directly to the Chairman...London three days per week...accommodation commensurate with...school fees until the age of 18...*

It's the best job offer I've ever received.

18.

Dubai
Five days to Closing

"Your Mr Tom is quite the wise guy, isn't he?"

I'm back at the old dhow wharf paying the Somali businessmen another visit. This time I'm on my own and the business is personal. We're going through the tea-drinking ritual again, but I'd rather just get on with what I've come for and leave.

"Yes, Mr Tom's a very wise guy indeed," I agree, accepting a second cup of the cardamom tea with an unsteady hand. I'd hoped my meditation this morning would settle me down, but when the yoga instructor had intoned, 'simply relax and observe the breath flowing effortlessly down your throat and into your lungs,' the very thought of my life depending on air passing through a tube the width of a coin had sent me into a mild panic. So here I am, frustratingly un-meditated and wishing it was this time next week.

"Wanker!" continues the Boss, sneering at me from the other side of the galley table.

Oh god, here we go, I think, *now I've got to explain Tom's password for the* Azusa *ransom payment and hope this guy shares his sense of humour.*

"The password worked out okay, then?" I enquire, dangerously close to choking on the last of my tea.

"The hawala agent in Mogadishu was highly offended by it. He was sure it was an insult directed at him personally."

"I am sorry to hear that, but that certainly wasn't Tom's intention," I say. "It's an acronym for *'Wife Away No Kids Eating Rubbish'*. Tom was thinking about expat family men – men like you, for instance – struggling through the summer in Dubai when their families go back home for the holidays. It's just his sense of humour."

"Wife away no kids eating rubbish?" the Boss repeats, staring at me and trying to decide if the joke's on him. "Very witty!" he eventually declares, grinning broadly. "Next time you see your Mr Tom, you tell him I like his sense of humour." He pauses briefly before adding, "But why insist on struggling alone through the summer like some sort of martyr?" He sounds genuinely perplexed at the thought. "I just send one of my wives to London with the kids and keep the other one here in Dubai to look after me. Problem solved!" he concludes, looking far too pleased with himself for my liking.

For this guy, having two wives is no more remarkable than having two high-end sports cars parked in the driveway. Slightly self-indulgent, maybe, but all perfectly normal nonetheless. It reminds me of a conversation I'd had with Tom just yesterday about the rights and wrongs of my own marital 'situation' and whether I should have done anything differently.

"What determines whether something is right or wrong anyway?" Tom had questioned. "The law? Religion? Public opinion? Because those three things are rarely aligned on anything. And then you throw different countries and cultures into the mix, and look what happens. Take issues such as abortion or capital punishment – there's a different verdict every which way you look. What you have done is bigamy. The United Kingdom says it's morally repugnant and a crime. Dubai says it's okay – provided you're a Muslim man, that is, and then you can have up to four wives. How can both of them be right?"

"Yeah, go figure," I'd replied, getting tetchier by the minute.

"But do you know why it's okay in Dubai for a Muslim man to have multiple wives?" Tom had ploughed on. "Because back in Prophet Muhammad's day, when a man's neighbour went off to battle and failed to come home, it was his moral duty to marry the widow so that she and the kids would be properly cared for. And the poor guy was expected to repeat this until his full quota of four wives had been filled. You may think it's wrong, and the laws of the UK may judge it to be wrong, but looked at this way, maybe Dubai is right on this issue? At its core, having multiple wives isn't anything to do with selfish greed or lust or anything like that, but about doing the right thing for others. Sound familiar?"

"Not really, to be honest. Unlike your good Muslim guy, I've been living a life of deceit and lying to everyone around me for the past three years."

"But what choice did you have? If you'd refused to marry Amal, you'd both have ended up on trial in Dubai for fornication, with your daughter as the prime evidence.

Instead, you married Amal and gave Noura a secure family environment, whilst also taking care of Josh at the same time. Forget what the law says, or religion, or public opinion or any of that. Surely it's the intentions behind the actions that should judge the rights and wrongs of your situation? What you have done isn't wrong, Chris, because you've done it for all the right reasons."

"That may be true," I'd replied, "but is that a sufficient defence? My conscience is still struggling with that one, I'm afraid."

"Then let's look at it this way," Tom had concluded with a grin, "you'd have been no help to anyone, especially your children, if you'd spent the last three years banged up in jail for your numerous crimes, whether here in Dubai or over in Britain."

Talking of banged up in jail, Tom had also told me the shocking truth about Amal and Lubna during our little conversation, and as soon as I get off this dhow I'm going to do something about it.

"Shall we get on with business?" I suggest to the Somali boss, suddenly conscious of the cramped confines and rising heat below the decks of *Heaven's Treasures*. "I need to get going." He snaps his fingers at one of his flunkeys who retrieves a large brown envelope from the shelf behind him and slides it across to me. I check the contents, pay the Boss in crisp dollar notes, as directed, and get out of there as quickly as possible.

"Good luck! I think you will need it," the Boss calls after me as I escape from the cabin and breathe in the glorious fresh, salty air up on deck. "And thanks for the business." *The smug bastard! It's alright for him with his neat*

*little domestic set up, all perfect and legal. That will be me next
time, if I get another chance.*

I'm walking back along the wharf as fast as I can
without drawing attention to myself when my mobile starts
to ring. It's Josh, but I already know that; my sixth sense
has warned me to expect his call. I connect to the sound
of my little boy's sobs wrapped around the news I had
been anticipating.

"Margo's gone!"

19.

Dubai

I feel bad for Josh but I can't be dealing with this right now. The clock's ticking and there's loads I still need to get done before Thursday. Next stop, the water taxi station further along the Creek. It's way too hot and humid to walk, plus Tom's waiting there already, so I jump in a cab for the two-minute journey.

"Just take us up to the Al Maktoum Bridge and back please, mate," Tom tells the driver as we step aboard an abra and make our way to the bow. The driver gives us a casual salute and throttles up the engine. A nifty reverse out of the dock and we're away, chugging through the choppy, brackish waters of the Creek, one vessel amongst dozens of others journeying in all directions through Dubai's liquid heart.

"This could be a *James Bond* movie," I say to Tom after a minute or two. "Very spies-and-villains-like."

"I thought we could do with getting some fresh air," he says, taking in the scene before turning to look directly at me. "But more importantly, there's no walls with ears out here on the water."

Tom's words are a blunt reminder of just how serious all this newly discovered shit with Amal is, a point easily forgotten amongst everything else going on at the moment.

"Should I really be doing this?" I'm scrutinizing Tom's face, reminding myself why I'm putting so much trust in this man at the moment. "It feels like a betrayal, to sell Amal down the river like this."

"You don't have a choice, Chris," Tom replies. "You need to be seen as cooperating, otherwise they'll be coming after you, too. How will it look if you disappear the very same week that Amal gets nabbed for money laundering?"

"And your guys are totally sure about this, are they?"

"I've told you, our financial crime team have received the full report from the Dubai CID. I've read it myself cover to cover. The investigation has been going on for months and there's no doubt: Just Jewels is about to be shut down across the region and everyone involved will be rounded up."

I'm studying Tom's face, this time searching for the emotion. *There it is*, I think, *anxiety raw as an open wound*. I look away and see we're approaching the old wharf I'd come from just fifteen minutes ago. A picture forms in my mind of the Al Zarounis' garden party last week, of armed police swarming in, handcuffing Amal and Lubna and hauling them away whilst the Al Zarouni seniors and their guests look on in stunned silence. *Imagine the shock! The shame! Christ, Amal, what have you done? To think I'd once had hope in you – that I'd thought marriage and parenthood would tame a restless spirit, that you would be there for Noura even if, some day in the future, I couldn't be. But our first and only trip away*

*as a family two years ago had put paid to any illusions in that
direction, hadn't it?*

"Let's go back to Cyprus for our wedding anniversary," I'd
suggested. "The three of us together."

The mention of 'three of us' had prompted a look of
surprise from Amal so I'd quickly added, "You, me and
Noura," before anything stupid was said. "It will be just
after her first birthday as well."

"Oh, yeah. Right. Do you really want to celebrate all
of that?"

"Yes, I think I do," I'd replied. "The last time we were
in Cyprus we were both in a state of shock. We'd just had a
baby we weren't planning to have and we were being forced
into a marriage neither of us wanted. I just think it might
help if we go back there again now, see if we can treat it as
a kind of fresh start for us all."

"Sure, why not. I could do with a break anyway."

So I went ahead and booked the trip. It was over a
weekend when Josh had a big karate competition going
on back in London and I really should have been there to
support him, but you can't change the date of anniversaries,
can you, they're immovable. We stayed at a winery up in the
Troodos mountains, one of those boutique resorts that was
once a traditional farming village, long-since abandoned
after an earthquake had shaken its tiny stone cottages, now
faithfully restored and converted into luxury guest suites.

Well, Amal quickly decided there were far more exciting
places to be that weekend. The scenery on the drive from the
airport that I found so enchanting – the vibrant blues of the
sea and sky, the greens of the olive groves and vineyards,
the rough and craggy coastline with its rocks sticking out

of the water like stepping stones for a giant, goats perched on chalky hillsides grazing on scrub, the sweeping birds (swallows or swifts?) – all of this beauty Amal just found 'bleak'.

And later that day sat on the winery's sunny terrace for a lunch that I found perfect – Greek salad drizzled with local olive oil, whole grilled sea bream sliced open and sprinkled with fresh herbs, succulent calamari, creamy halloumi and the freshest tzatziki, served up with a carafe of chilled Xynisteri – all of this just didn't hit the mark either. Apparently the food 'wasn't as good as the Lebanese meze' and the wine was only 'okay if you like *plonk*, as I think you Brits call it'.

"Let's go for a walk," I'd suggested after lunch. So the three of us had set off along a goat trail above the village, Amal striding ahead in a rush to get it over with, and me taking my time with Noura, pointing out the carobs, beehives, butterflies, almond blossom, when a scream of "Arghhhh, snake, snake!" suddenly pierced the air and Amal came bounding back to join us. "Honestly, what a fuss," I'd said. "It's just a grass snake, we get these in the West Country all the time," and I'd flicked it away with a stick.

Things didn't get any better that evening. Lubna called whilst we were having dinner: I knew it was her from the way Amal had said 'hey' and had gone outside into the cobbled lane to continue the conversation. A couple of strangers threw admiring glances as they passed by and I remember seeing Amal through their eyes, so confidently attractive and oozing with style. And I realised I was no longer attracted. Simple as that. We went to bed that night in stony silence and in the morning Amal was gone, a scribbled note 'Gone to Beirut for urgent business' left on the bedside table. I'd rushed into the adjoining room, fearful Noura was gone too (my dark angel at it again) but the only other thing missing was the hire car and I'd had to get the chambermaid's cousin to drop us back at the airport later that day in his rattly old farm truck.

On the flight back to Dubai I'd googled 'swifts or swallows' and settled on swallows, owing to their long, forked tails. I'd also googled Cyprus snakes whilst I was at it and, bugger me, that 'grass snake' we'd come across on our walk was actually a blunt-nosed viper, 'the most venomous snake on the island and potentially fatal to humans'. Whoops!

After that trip, although nothing was actually said, there had been an understanding between Amal and me that we weren't meant to be together. I should have ended it back then, but I'd had nowhere to take my daughter and I wasn't about to leave her with Amal and the Al Zarounis.

So here I am, two years later, sat on an abra and having this uncomfortable conversation with Tom.

"It all started back in January 2018 with a bunch of Indian jewel thieves crashing their getaway vehicle into the side of a police cruiser on the Riyadh to Jeddah highway," Tom continues. "The thieves were arrested and interviewed, and this led to a multi-agency investigation across the Gulf region and the eventual rounding up of a jewellery theft ring that had stolen millions of dollars' worth of jewellery in fifteen separate heists across Saudi, Bahrain, Kuwait and the United Arab Emirates."

We're passing the old dhow wharf now, and I focus on spotting *Heaven's Treasures* berthed amongst all the other wooden dhows in the wharf. *Ah, there she is, hiding in plain sight, her decks empty and quiet...*

"They were a well-organised enterprise, operating in small groups that targeted jewellery stores in the souqs and other older parts of their chosen cities. Some of the group would distract sales and security personnel, while others acted as lookouts. Once they were ready to proceed, a few of them would stand around a showcase to shield it from view while others used a tool to cut the silicone holding the case together and removed all the jewellery. The group would then flee to a waiting getaway vehicle."

"But how does this relate to Just Jewels?" I must be honest, I'm still struggling to reconcile the Amal I thought I knew (the self-centred, commitment-phobic, but nonetheless harmless ratbag) with this entirely sinister version that's unveiling before me.

"The thieves needed to turn the jewellery into cash, and Just Jewels was there to help them with that. A full confession from one of the ring leaders, obtained in return for a more lenient time of things, led the investigation straight to Just Jewels' door. Amal and Lubna have been buying the stolen jewellery from the thieves, you see. At prices well below their market value, of course. It's what's known in the game as 'fencing'.

Once the investigators really get to work on Just Jewels, they'll probably find that Amal and Lubna have been buying jewels cheaply from a number of other illegal sources as well – animal poachers and drug dealers paid in diamonds, company executives bribed with gold."

I'm feeling pretty queasy by now and I don't think it's the motion of the boat.

"But that's unlikely to be the whole story," Tom continues. "It's suspected Just Jewels will also be involved with on-selling the stolen jewellery to criminals needing to exchange their dirty money for gold, diamonds and other less traceable forms of currency. Amal and Lubna will be part of a circle of crime, buying jewels cheap from one lot of criminals and selling them on to other criminals at inflated prices, making a more-than-tidy profit in the process."

"I must admit," I tell him, "what I found in Amal's safe last night supports what you're saying."

Tom's eyebrows instantly shoot up and amusement trembles the corners of his mouth. "Safe-breaking, eh? Was that an elective at your law school, then, or is it a skill you've just happened to pick up along the way?"

"Sorry to disappoint, Tom, but all I did was punch in Amal's date of birth and press *unlock*. Bingo! It was the first combination I tried."

"Geez."

"I know: the arrogant little shit is completely impervious to the risk of being caught. It's all sat in that safe, just waiting to be found. I counted more than six hundred thousand dollars in cash, plus the dirhams, rials and so on. There must be around a million in total in there. There's a mobile phone too, with maybe twenty or thirty names listed in the contacts."

"Great! Fresh leads for the investigators. This little racket of Amal's has been going on for years. The legitimate Just Jewels business that we all see, the glitzy stores in fancy locations, is just a front for the money-laundering operation going on behind the scenes. Just Jewels is all about fair trade, ethics? That's a joke. And whatever Amal's father might like to think, this is no thirty-year-old guilt keeping

Amal glued to Lubna's side, either; they're partners in crime and they're both up to their eyeballs in filth."

Tom's only told me what I already know – I've sat through enough anti-money laundering refresher courses during my career to understand how it all works – but any lingering shreds of doubt about whether all this could apply to Amal have now gone. This is worse than anything I could ever be accused of. Much, much worse. It's bereft of any moral purpose. It's crime with a capital 'C'. And I'm bloody sickened by it. I take an envelope out of my jacket pocket. "My statement," I say, handing it to Tom. "I've included everything I can think of that might be relevant: where Amal's safe is hidden and the combination to access it, the password for the mobile – no prizes for guessing that one, either – all our bank account details, anything and everything I can remember about Amal and Lubna's circle of friends and contacts, I've written it all down."

"Good work, Chris. This statement will show the authorities what side you're on, that you've got nothing to do with Amal's crimes," Tom says, slotting the envelope into his bag. "Things are about to turn ugly, and you're getting out just in time."

20.

Sunday 3rd October, 1999

At long last I've managed to escape from Bristol again and I'm back at Uni to start my second year. What a relief.

I can say it now it's over – Summer was bloody awful. I am never going to work in a supermarket again (especially stacking shelves and working the till – what a sad bloody cliché) and I'm done with spending every spare moment living at my mother's whim.

This time last year I thought I could escape my past, move on, have a fresh start. How naïve was that!!!

But that's it now, I'm done. It's time to live my life the way I want.

Sorry Journal, but since I can't put it all in a box and forget about it, you are going to have to hear it. It will be cathartic.

*

Thursday 7th October, 1999

I saw a father in the corner shop with his two kids this
afternoon. He was helping them choose their 20p's
worth of sweets and it made me think about my own
dad. He left home when I was nine. He was sent down
the corner shop for nappies and cigarettes one evening
and just never came back.

*

Wednesday 17th November, 1999

From my Criminal Law lecture this morning:
Theft Act 1968, Clause 1: Basic definition of theft
(1) A person is guilty of theft if he dishonestly
appropriates property belonging to another with the
intention of permanently depriving the other of it; and
"thief" and "steal" shall be construed accordingly.
(2) It is immaterial whether the appropriation is made
with a view to gain, or is made for the thief's own benefit.

From my memory bank:
Mum was at work and I was looking after Ryan. This
was about a year after Dad had left, because Mum was
working evenings and Ryan was at the crawling stage.
It was tea time but there was nothing to eat and Ryan
was getting tetchy. We went to the mini supermarket on
the high street run by the Clarksons to get some food. I
stashed it all in Ryan's buggy and we went home.

I didn't pay for it because we didn't have any money.

I didn't intend to permanently deprive Mr and Mrs Clarkson of those yogurts and pies – in my mind I was somehow going to pay for them later, when I could. But that doesn't make it any better.

I'm feeling deeply ashamed of myself all over again.

Bloody Mum!

*

Friday January 14th, 2000

A few of us went down the pub this evening and we were exchanging stories about all the horrible things our parents did to us when we were growing up. Alison said she was scarred for life because her mum once threw up on the cat after getting drunk on her dad's rum punch and she'd had to clean it up. Andrew's dad once choked on a toffee on a train and he'd had to do the Heimlich manoeuvre on him, resulting in the toffee shooting out of his dad's mouth and straight down a woman's cleavage. Big bloody deal.

I didn't contribute to this discussion because I couldn't think of any funny stories to tell that were on the right side of acceptable. Imagine the reaction around the table if I'd told everyone about the time Mum had stayed in bed for three straight months and we'd had to rely on the kindness of neighbours to get us all through it. Mrs Robins on the left looked after Ryan whilst I was at school and Mrs Clarke on the right let herself in during the day to see to Mum and do some tidying up.

I handled all the family finances during that time, and I saw for myself just how hand-to-mouth our existence was. Going to the post office each week to draw out cash and get Postal Orders to pay the bills, keeping a running total of the groceries in my head as I went around the supermarket, making sure there were enough fifty pence coins to keep the electric meter in the coat cupboard fed.

I calculated that twenty percent of our household income went on Mum's fags.

I believed Mum when she told me it was glandular fever that kept her in bed. Now when I look back on that time, I'm pretty sure it was depression.

Anyway, it's not really something I'd want to share with everybody down the pub.

*

Thursday 17th February, 2000

We were asked to debate the pro's and con's of abortion in our Comparative Law seminar today.

Here's what I think:

Mum met a new guy about three years after Dad left. He was a plumber and he'd come to fix a leak in our bathroom. I remember he came around the day after to check everything was okay with the repair and Mum offered him a cup of tea.

He was a really nice guy, Keith, and whilst the relationship lasted I held out hope we'd found our knight in shining armour. But he just vanished out of our lives one day, I'm not sure why, and then Mum found out she was pregnant.

I had to be her sounding board, because there was no adult around to listen to her – she didn't have any close friends, she was estranged from her sister and the neighbours' helpfulness was strictly practical. So I heard about how Keith had led her on, then dumped her without any reason, that he was as bad as my father, they're all the same, and it's always the woman left with the problem and should she have an abortion, could we manage with another child in the house, perhaps she'd be able to get more family support, and so on.

I didn't have answers to any of this. Why would I? I was 12 years old.

Mum had the abortion and at the time I felt sad.

Now I just feel relieved.

So I think it's right that there's a choice.

*

Wednesday 22nd March, 2000

Mum told me on the phone today she was surprised I was getting on so well at Uni. A tad passive-aggressive I think, but it's still progress. When I'd first told her two years ago that I was going to University she'd slapped my face. Her hand just came out of nowhere and Wham! I'd told her I thought she'd be pleased, proud of me even. She'd told me she didn't understand me and she'd lit up another cigarette even though there was already one burning in the ashtray.

The first day I'd left on the train to come to Uni, Mum was like pure venom. She'd said I was doing it to spite her and that I was in for a big fall when I failed.

*

Thursday 6th April, 2000

Q: Why on earth would I be thinking about Christmas at this time of year?

A: Because I heard a lady on the bus today talking about her grandson who has already written to father Christmas and put in his request for a Pokémon game before the shops run out of them.

Anyway, it reminded me of that Christmas Mum went around the neighbours for pre-lunch drinks, didn't get home until about 5pm and put herself straight to bed. We didn't see her again until Boxing Day.

Ryan and I spent the afternoon watching telly, waiting for her to come home and put the Christmas lunch on. In the end, I cooked the Christmas lunch for dinner and we ate it on our laps watching *Star Wars*.

When Mum surfaced on Boxing Day she said she was sorry, the neighbours had given her too much to drink.

That was the first and last time she's ever apologised for anything.

*

Friday 26th May, 2000

I had my Land Law exam this morning so I'm half way through them already. This time next Friday, I'll have finished the second year of Uni.

Two down, one to go. I'm over the hump!

I'm going to Bristol for the Summer again, but not to be at Mum's beck and call this time. This time, I'm doing it for Ryan. Since I found out last week about his diabetes I've spoken to one of the med students and put together a treatment plan for us to follow:

1. Meals – cut out sugary and fast foods, replace with fresh vegetables, fruit and whole grains. Try out different recipes whilst I'm there and leave Mum with a weekly grocery list and meal list.
2. Exercise – find free sports for kids and work out a daily/weekly fitness schedule with Ryan. Get him some cool new kit to wear.
3. Insulin injections or pump? Get the doctor's advice.
4. Establish a daily routine for them both to check/correct blood sugar levels.
5. Get Ryan an 'I've got Type 1 diabetes' pendant to wear.

Mum needs to get her act together with this and she'd better not balls it up.

21.

Dubai
Three days to Closing

"I understand some of the due diligence documents haven't been uploaded to the data room yet?"

We're in Mark's office on the forty-first floor of Emirates Towers going through the final arrangements for the sale of Bailey's Dubai which is due to close in three days' time. I can't quite look Mark in the eye so I focus out the window instead. Three window cleaners are dangling off ropes from the skyscraper opposite, their swing seats and buckets looking far too flimsy for the task. In the distance, the Arabian Gulf glistens tantalisingly in the late-afternoon sun. *I want to be out there, on one of those fancy white yachts, or even a cargo ship would do, provided it's headed somewhere away from here.*

"What's going on?" Mark demands, forcing me to look directly at him. "When we spoke on the phone last week you promised me there'd be no snags, that everything was on track to close as planned. I've exchanged contracts on the casino land now."

"Oh Mark, I thought you'd slowed that one down? You know I'm worried about you being able to get the gambling license in place."

"I appreciate your concern but I'm already talking to a license holder in Margate who's willing to sell, so things are moving well on that front."

"But that's just the first step, you then need the Gambling Commission to..."

"Yes, I know all of that, but I've laid out five million quid already on the casino project, I'm past the point of no return and, as you well know, I'm relying on the Bailey's Dubai sale to fund construction."

Yes, Mark, I know that only too well. I focus my gaze back on the three dangling window cleaners and hear the blood swooshing through my ears to the rhythm of my amplified heartbeat.

I wonder if their wives worry about them doing that job every day?

Slow breath in.

The money must be worth it, I guess?

Slow breath out.

Oh god, I hope Mark's going to go along with this.

"Without those assignment releases Al Shamsi will be looking to re-open the deal and bag himself a bargain. I've seen these games before. He'll say there's a risk that money's still owed to the banks on the construction, which we all know is complete bullshit, but he'll have me by the short and curlies, won't he?"

He's scrutinizing my face intently now, trying to gauge my reaction no doubt, and hoping his frustration isn't about to morph into disappointment, that I'm going to present a plausible explanation for all of this and make everything all right again. It's time for me to come clean, but this is not going to be an easy conversation.

Twenty-four sheets of paper, eighteen signatures, twelve corporate seals, six staples, simply thrown into the bin this morning for my five hundred thousand dollars and near-perfect job. As simple as that. But Josh, Noura, Mark, Tom – they all deserve better, don't they? I retrieved those documents from the trash, and now here I am.

"Mark," I begin, "there's a few things I need to tell you. I'm sorry, you're not going to like what you're about to hear but the truth is, I haven't always been entirely honest with you."

I watch as his eyes narrow by the slightest fraction and his mouth drops at the corners. The beginnings of disappointment. "Go on," he says.

"You know I'm married to Alex, right?"

"Yes, of course."

I take a deep breath before going on. "Well, I'm also married to someone here in Dubai, to Amal Al Zarouni, part of the Al Zarouni family. We have a daughter, Noura. She's three."

On the positive side, I can only tell you that Mark's expression at this point isn't one of disappointment: it's more the stunned look of a man who thought he'd heard it all before only to find out there's a whole extra layer of life out there he had no idea existed.

"So, you see," I say, keen to plough on, "I'm a bigamist. I have two families, one in London and the other here in Dubai. I'm sorry to have shocked you. No doubt you're wondering what else I've been hiding from you over the years – and whether you can trust me anymore."

"Well..."

"I can only hope that when you hear the full story, you will understand I had no real choice. It's not something I planned or am proud of and I'd rather you'd never had to know anything about it, but here we are."

"So why are you telling me now?"

"Shamal Enterprises have found out. Remember that meeting we had in Al Shamsi's boardroom a few weeks back? The all-nighter?"

"How could I forget?"

"Well, Haddad recognized me as one of the other parents from my daughter's nursery school. His son is in the same class as Noura so we'd crossed paths a few times. Then you happened to mention to him that our families were close back in London, that you'd attended my wedding a few years ago, and he worked the rest out from there."

"I hope you're not blaming me for this, Chris! How the hell would I know I can't open my mouth without landing you into trouble? I may have big balls, but they ain't made of crystal, you know." Mark inhales audibly, causing his nostrils to flare in a manner completely unfamiliar to me, then he closes his eyes and slowly exhales. "So, *has* it landed you into trouble with him?"

"Actually, it's landed us both into trouble" I reply, focused on keeping my tone calm. "And this is all entirely my fault."

I pour us both a glass of water, take a sip from mine and sit back in my chair, giving Mark a minute to digest everything. The proverbial penny doesn't take long to drop: "The bastards!" he shouts, slamming his hand on the table and making his water spill. "They're trying to use this to their advantage in the Bailey's sale, aren't they?"

"By bribing me to sabotage the due diligence," I confirm, nodding. "They promised to keep my *situation* secret in return for me *losing* the conditional land assignment releases. And yes, they saw this as a way of batting you down on the Bailey's Dubai sale price at the eleventh hour. Blimey, they even tried to sweeten the deal by offering me half a million dollars and a job with Shamal Enterprises, working between Dubai and London so I could keep hopping between my two families."

"The fact you're telling me all this now must mean you've decided not to go along with their plan?" I'm relieved to hear hope returning to Mark's voice.

"I've had no choice but to go along with their plan up until now, otherwise they'd have squealed on me already. If I'd uploaded those *lost* due diligence documents to the data room they'd have wasted no time sharing their lucky discovery of my bigamy with both my families, not to mention leading me straight into the hands of Bad Cop."

"Bad Cop, who's that?"

Bad Cop. This character has been such a constant torment to me over the last three years I forget sometimes that she isn't actually real. "I'm just speaking figuratively," I tell Mark. "You know, it's actually a relief to be telling you all this, sharing it with you at last. It's been a difficult three years."

"To be honest, I didn't notice anything, Chris; you've always seemed perfectly fine to me. Reliable. On the ball. How did you manage to keep going on as normal through all of that?"

"Everything may have looked normal from the outside, but inside I was a complete mess. For those first few months after Noura was born and I was pressured into marrying

Amal, I was numb, just dragging myself through each day, and from one continent to the other. It took me months to accept my new family situation in Dubai, whilst at the same time I was neglecting Josh. It all seemed pretty hopeless for a while, but things slowly settled into a routine of sorts. I managed to get my act together and was coping pretty well. Until the last few weeks, that is. The sale of Bailey's Dubai really shook things up again."

"Hmm, I can see why a role with Shamal Enterprises would seem appealing to you. Losing those documents for Al Shamsi would be a simple solution. Why not just go along with it?"

"I wouldn't stab you in the back, you know that." I try to sound as earnest as I can but it comes out sounding fake. "Besides, you know I don't *lose* documents." This is rewarded with a wry smile from Mark. "Just think, if I'd gone along with their plan, the risk of them exposing me at any moment would be hanging over my head forever. They'd own me. And to be honest, I don't want to live this lie anymore; I'm tired of running backwards and forwards, juggling all the responsibilities, trying to keep it all going. Both my marriages are loveless anyway, so what's the point? I've had enough of it, and now that my role here in Dubai is coming to an end, it's a good time for me to sort out my life. I need to move on."

I look at Mark and catch a momentary glimpse of the frail old man I'd first noticed back in Al Shamsi's boardroom those few weeks ago. I feel terrible for putting him through all this and I lean across to give his arm a reassuring squeeze.

"I couldn't accept their bribe, for your sake or mine, so instead I had to find a way to turn the tables on them. From the moment Haddad grabbed my arm as I was leaving that meeting and told me, 'I know what you are,' I was on notice of a problem in the making, so I started keeping records."

I dig into my briefcase, pull out a document and slide it across to Mark. "Transcripts of the text messages Haddad sent me after that first meeting."

Mark reads the sheet, "*I believe you have a personal dilemma we can usefully discuss. Call me,* sent on June 10th at 20.53. *Time is running out if we're to do something about that personal dilemma of yours,* sent on June 16th at 09.40."

"Shows intimidation. But there's more, much more." I pull out two photos and hand them to Mark. "Haddad sent these to me. The first one of Josh and me came by WhatsApp with the message 'happy families number 1'. He was stalking me in London. The second one was taken in Dubai."

Mark gazes at the photo of Noura and me flying the kite together. "Happy families number two," he reads, turning it over. "This must be your daughter?"

"Yep, and that photo arrived by courier to my house in Pimlico last week. Josh saw it." Mark raises his eyebrows. "Yes, that was awkward, to say the least. It came with this." I hand Mark the job offer from Shamal Enterprises, which he briefly skims and places with the photos.

"Anyway," I continue, "all this is just circumstantial fluff. Here's the real evidence." I locate an audio file on my phone and press play. The full recording is eight minutes long, but the crucial phrases stand out, '*...the lawyer on the other side is less than straight. 'Bigamy,' that's what it's called... help each other out here...think about how your two families would react...very convenient indeed if you failed to fulfil all of our due diligence requirements...*'

Mark looks utterly appalled, but manages to remain tight-lipped as he listens to the electronic whine of Haddad's voice.

...reduced price...make sure you're adequately compensated for your efforts...half a million dollars...this can be a 'win-win' situation...'.

"The devious little shit!" he exclaims at the end.

"And here's another one." I press play again. *'...grand enough for you...or perhaps it would be* families *in your case... married into the Al Zarouni family...all know what's going on with each other...nothing to tarnish their reputation...offer you a position here at Shamal Enterprises...we need a negotiating tool and that's where you come in...get me that ten million reduction, and as far as I'm concerned you're part of my team...'.*

"Blackmail, bribery, attempted conspiracy to defraud: it's all there," I say. "And here's something a little extra." I slide another photo across the desk to Mark. "This one was taken just last week, by a private investigator I hired. Great action shot, I thought." The photo is of Al Shamsi looking very dapper in the back of a London cab, but what's interesting about this photo is not where he is or what he's wearing – it's who he's with and what he's doing to them. "That's definitely not his wife," I tell Mark, allowing myself the briefest of smiles. "For you to keep as insurance, just in case. And I have one more thing for you," I say, retrieving an A4-sized envelope from my briefcase and pushing it across the desk. Mark opens it and pulls out a bundle of legal documents.

"Let me guess," he says. "The *lost* assignment releases?"

"Correct. Now let me explain how this is all going to work."

22.

Dubai
Closing Day

I'm booked on the nine-forty flight to Heathrow this morning and this time Noura's coming with me. Today's the day we're going to disappear. Amal wasn't at home last night, away on some dubious 'business' trip, so it was easy enough to get a case packed for Noura and me. The only slight hiccup was when Rose made an appearance as I was packing the last of Noura's things. She asked if I was taking Noura to London with me this time and I told her I was just sorting out some old clothes for a charity drive at work. An unlikely story, but it was the best I could come up with on the spot. I think it worked though, because she just said 'goodnight' and took herself off to bed, and this morning she was business as usual, giving us breakfast and helping us get out the door and into the waiting taxi, suitcase and all.

As far as Noura's concerned, today has started off like many others – with me dropping her off at nursery school on my way to catch a flight – and she's sitting quite happily, watching the outside world zip by. I check my watch: plenty of time to get to the airport, provided we don't run into any holdups along the way.

I pick a moment when we're cruising comfortably down the Sheikh Zayed Road to plant the first seeds of the plan with my little travel companion. "Hey Noura!" I exclaim in my most excited would-you-believe-it-I've-just-had-the-most-amazing-lightbulb-moment-whilst-whizzing-along-this-road voice. "Why don't we go flying in a big plane today? You know, one of those double-deckers where we can sit upstairs?"

Noura's eyes open as wide as saucers as she considers all the possibilities such an idea might offer. "I wouldn't have to go to nursery today?" she enquires tentatively.

"Nope, no nursery."

"What about cartoons? Can I still watch cartoons today?"

"Yes, you can watch Barmy Charlie and all your other favourites onboard the airplane."

"Where will we fly to?"

"London. It's a new city you haven't been to before. The Queen of England lives there."

"And Prince George."

"Yes, and Prince George. It's all going to be very exciting, just wait and see."

"Mmmm. So, what about people?"

"What *about* people?"

"How many other people will there be on the plane?"

"Erm, eight hundred or so?"

"And they're going to let *us* fly it?"

"Erm, no, they've got professional pilots for that, Noura. But you can eat your lunch on board," I add quickly. "No yucky school food today."

"Yessss!" she squeals, giving me a high five. "We are going to be in *sooo* much trouble when we get home." And with that, she starts singing her own little song about going on an airplane with all the grown-ups and cartoon animals to visit Prince George and eating only Jaffa Cakes and Hobnobs all day instead of going to yucky nursery school. *Just the reaction I was hoping for.* I go to check my phone and have a moment of panic when I find it missing from its usual slot in my bag. *Of course, you dimwit! You left it with Tom last night. You're using cash to pick up a new mobile in duty-free and then getting a SIM card when we land at Heathrow. Relax, it's all under control... God, I hope there are no holdups on the road today!*

I usually use the Smart Gates to get through passport control and I'm tempted to chance using them now. *If I carry Noura through perhaps nobody will notice her and I can avoid her being checked by immigration altogether? No, that's a dumb idea, Chris. You've already thought all this through. Just stick to the plan and nothing will go wrong.* I eye the long line of white-robed immigration officers seated back-to-back at their counters checking passengers' passports and join the queue. I've got our passports tightly gripped in one hand – mine worn and crumpled and Noura's shiny and stiff – and I'm holding Noura close to my side with the other. I'm doing my new deep-breathing thing (*in slowly, two, three, four, five, out slowly, two, three, four, five, six*) but it's not helping much because my heart's still booming like a bass drum at five times the speed of my breathing and I'm forced to take a huge gulp of air to catch up with it. I'm trying to control a rising fear that despite me taking Noura out on a British passport, the immigration department's computer system will still somehow identify her as a UAE national. *They use iris identification and goodness knows what else nowadays. They'll never let me take her out of the country if they know she's Emirati.*

Try to focus on our next steps. In a minute we'll reach the head of the queue and then we'll walk across to the next free counter. It will be that immigration officer over there, the friendly-looking one who's having a laugh with his colleague. He'll carry on chatting to his colleague as we stand in front of him and he'll take no particular interest in us. He'll just glance over the top of the counter at Noura and then at me as he checks our boarding passes and waves our passports in front of his scanner. He'll watch his computer screen and I'll watch him, looking for any tell-tale twitch of facial muscle to signal that we've been busted. He'll look away from the screen and pick up his stamp – thump, thump, *that glorious sound – and he'll slide the two passports back to me.*

'Shukran,' I'll say, 'thank you', and Noura and I will pass through passport control and take the short train journey to Concourse A. I'll check the information board and our flight will be there, shown as being on time and boarding in twenty minutes from Gate A3, so we'll whizz through duty-free, picking up a cheap Nokia phone and a pair of fluffy camels as we go, the big one for Josh and the smaller one for Noura, which she'll kiss on the head and hug tightly to her chest as we make our way to the boarding gate.

We'll be welcomed aboard the plane by a posse of smiling flight attendants milling around the cabin door and we'll find our seats six rows down on the left: a window for Noura and an aisle for me. I'll fasten Noura's seatbelt around her and her camel and then I'll fasten my own as the Captain will chime over the address system, 'Good morning ladies and gentleman, girls and boys, and welcome aboard this Emirates flight to Heathrow.

*My name is Blankety Blank, and I have the pleasure of flying you to London today. Air traffic control have confirmed an on-time departure for us, so we're just waiting for the last pieces of luggage to be loaded on board and we'll be on our way. Cruising altitude is thirty-six thousand feet and the weather along the route is expected to be smooth and clear. We should have you on the ground at Heathrow by two-forty this afternoon, where the weather is forecast to be dry and sunny with the temperature hovering around a balmy eighteen degrees Celsius. Blimpety Blimp is your chief flight attendant today, and he and his team will be taking great care of you all. So it just remains for me to say thank you for choosing to fly with Emirates and sit back, relax and enjoy the flight. I'll now hand you over to Blimpety Blimp…'
And Blimpety Blimp will smoothly pick up from where Captain Blankety Blank left off. '…We now ask for your attention whilst we show you a short safety video…,' but by then Noura and I will be engrossed in our own little inflight entertained worlds and we won't hear when Blimpety Blimp asks all ground personnel to please leave the aircraft, thank you, and for the cabin crew to prepare all doors and cross-check.*

Noura will look excitedly out the window as the aircraft rumbles over the tarmac towards the runway whilst cabin crew pass briskly down the aisles issuing orders: all window blinds must be open; seats must be in their upright position; hand luggage must be securely stowed; overhead lockers must be firmly shut. 'Cabin crew, take your seats for takeoff,' Captain Blankety Blank will then request and the engines will power up, sending vibrations juddering down the plane. When we reach the start of the runway the airplane will shudder more violently as the engines are brought up to full power and the aircraft will begin its lumber down the runway, slowly at first but gathering speed as it eats up the dotted white lines faster and faster towards our take off. The rumble underfoot and the shaking of lockers overhead will disappear the instant the aircraft leaves the tarmac and begins its steep ascent. After a few minutes the engines will slow to a quiet background hum and the flaps will retreat as the plane continues its gentle climb. We'll be passing through dense white cloud and it will feel as if we're sliding back, slowly, slowly...

My ears suddenly tighten at the sound of multiple footsteps approaching from behind and I feel the prickle of goosebumps shimmy down my arms as I'm grabbed firmly on the shoulder and hear the words I've dreaded hearing at every airport over the last three years:

"Chris Jones, please come with us."

23.

Dubai

That didn't go too well, did it? We only left home an hour ago and I've been caught already! My mobile's with Tom, the very person I need to call, and they won't lend me one of theirs; 'no need,' I was told with a dismissive wave of the hand. I tried explaining that there must be some kind of mistake, that I've done nothing wrong and they should just let Noura and me get on our way, but that didn't work. So here we are, stuck in this side room and being watched over by an adolescent policeman going by the name of Officer Omar Al Hamdy.

"I need to use the bathroom," Noura says, twisting in my lap to whisper in my ear. I look across the desk at Al Hamdy and shrug my shoulders as if to say, *What can you do? When they've got to go, they've got to go.* "I need to take my daughter to the bathroom," I tell him. "Which way is it?"

"No problem," he says, rising from his chair, "but she goes and you must wait here." He strides across the room, opens the door and shouts, "Amina! Come!" There's a brief silence and then we hear heavy footsteps thumping down the corridor and a portly policewoman comes rushing into the room, red-faced and out of breath from her ten-yard sprint. "Take the girl to the bathroom," Al Hamdy tells her, and then issues more instructions in a rapid-fire Arabic that's well beyond my level of comprehension. WPC Weeble smiles thinly at Noura, grabs her by the arm and tugs her off my lap.

I just can't shake the thought that this is it; they're taking her off me. "No!" I shout, jumping to my feet as Noura's led away. "You can't take her."

"Sit down. Relax. Everything will be fine, inshallah," says Al Hamdy, settling himself in his chair.

How will everything be fine? That evil battle-axe has just taken my daughter away! What if that's it and I never get to see her again? I'm going to be banged up in jail and then deported. I'll be deleted from her life. Zap! Gone forever! The Al Zarounis will make sure of it.

"Would you like something to drink, perhaps? Coffee? Tea?"

You've got to be kidding me.

A Talking Heads song chooses to pop into my mind at this point, one I haven't heard in years... *And you may find yourself in another part of the world...*

"No, I don't want a drink!" I say as firmly and calmly as I can. "I want my daughter back and then I want you to let us go."

And you may find yourself in a beautiful house, with a beautiful wife...

"You've got plenty of time, just relax. There's some dates if you're hungry?"

And you may ask yourself, well, how did I get here?

More to the point, how the hell am I going to get out *of here?*

"At least let me make a phone call. I have the right to a phone call."

"Okay, okay," says Al Hamdy, putting his hands up in surrender. "Here, use my phone."

"Thank you."

Right, let's get Tom over here.

I delve into my bag and pull out the envelope that was given to me by the Somali businessmen earlier this week – I've written Tom's mobile number under the flap – and as I go to place it on the desk, three crisp green passports slide out of the envelope. Then everything happens all at once: Noura comes skipping back into the room after her trip to the loo, enthusiastically waving an Emirati flag on a stick as Al Hamdy goes to reach across the table to grab the passports but instead leaps to his feet and salutes to a very officious-looking senior police officer who enters the room and yells, "Chris Jones? Yallah, let's go." According to his name badge, this is Major Hussain Jaziri, and according to his manner, he's not a man to mess with.

"We're ready for you now. Come this way."

Yikes! I feel my cheeks prickle from the sudden surge of blood to my face.

I quickly gather up my papers and shove them back in my bag, grab Noura's hand and run to catch up with the Major, who's already out the door and marching down the corridor.

"Miss Al Nuaimi sends her best regards," he says as Noura and I catch up with him.

"Can you repeat that, please?" I say, because I surely couldn't have heard that right.

"Miss Al Nuaimi," he insists. "She asked me to convey her best wishes to you."

"Are you talking about *Lubna* Al Nuaimi?" I ask.

"Yes, of course. I understand she's a very good friend of yours?"

"We've got close family connections," I say, immediately worrying I've said too much and this admission is going to ruin any chances of freedom. After all, she's recently become a wanted criminal.

"Very close, I would think," says Jaziri. "She's asked me to escort you through the airport this morning. I hope my colleagues treated you well whilst you were waiting?"

How the hell did Lubna know I was planning to leave with Noura today?

The long, straight corridor he leads us down has a row of offices on one side and windows running along the other, giving us a view through to the check-in and passport control areas where Noura and I were apprehended just fifty minutes ago. *Rose must have figured out what was happening and told her cousin who told Lubna.* We've walked past the Smart Gates and the line of immigration officers sat at their counters, and now we're walking past the security area where our hand luggage should be checked. But no, we're bypassing all of it. *Go to jail. Go directly to jail. Do not pass Go. Do not even think about collecting anything from duty-free. Where the hell is this guy taking us?* My heart's flip-flopping around my rib cage like a fish in a bucket, I'm that panicked.

"She asked me to give you this," the Major says, stopping abruptly and delving into his inside jacket pocket.

"Excuse me?"

He passes me a sealed envelope with my name written on the front in bold purple pen. "It's a letter from Miss Al Nuaimi," he says. I'm tempted to rip the envelope open and read the contents immediately – perhaps it will shed some light on what's going on – but I'm told by the Major that I'm to 'read it on the plane'.

"Plane?" I say.

"You were planning to fly to London today, weren't you?"

"Well, yes. We're booked on the nine-forty to Heathrow, actually."

"Indeed you are," he replies cryptically, before turning on his heels and continuing to march down the corridor.

We're taken by police buggy through a series of empty back tunnels, the Major sat up front with the driver and Noura and me sat behind. The stark white tiles on the walls flash blue from the overhead fluorescent lights as we whizz along, taking a left turn here and a right turn there until – *dare I believe it?* – we exit the final tunnel straight into the daylight of an empty departure lounge.

"Please enjoy your flight," says the Major, leading us to the airbridge and shaking my hand. "They're ready to depart as soon as you're on board."

And indeed, we're welcomed aboard the A380 by smiling flight attendants waiting for us at the cabin door and we're shown to our seats, six rows down on the left: a window for Noura and an aisle for me. I fasten Noura's seatbelt and then I fasten my own as the Captain chimes over the address system, "Good morning ladies and gentleman, girls and boys, and welcome aboard this Emirates flight to Heathrow. My name is Greg Stewart..."

I sit back, take a large swig of the champagne that's just been given to me with orders to 'drink it quick, we're preparing for takeoff', tear open the envelope and take out a folded sheet of paper. On it is scrawled this message:

I've got you and your brat out of the country. Now both of you piss off and don't come back. LAN.

Cheers, Lubna!

24.

Tuesday 10th October, 2000

So here I am, at the start of my third and final year at Uni.

This is crunch time. I need to get my head down and go for it this year. Tough assessment deadlines to meet and final exams to pass, plus I need to get a training contract with a law firm.

I need to prove I can be a lawyer and then I need to earn money doing it.

Otherwise it's over to Plan B. Photography. Photojournalism maybe?

I've left Ryan in a good place with his diabetes treatment plan. Mum and he just need to follow it properly.

I've agreed with Ryan that one day he will come and live with me, just as soon as I've got my own place and I'm earning enough to keep us both.

I'm doing this for the two of us now.

*

Thursday 26th October, 2000

I called home to check on Ryan earlier this evening. He wasn't there so Mum picked up. She was slurring her words which makes me think she's hit the bottle again. I'll need to keep an eye on that.

She says she's been checking Ryan's blood sugar levels though, and that they're ok.

Do I need to go down there this weekend to check everything for myself?

I'll wait and see what Ryan says when he calls me back later.

*

Friday 27th October, 2000

I called home again and managed to get hold of Ryan this time. He says he's fine and he sounds happy enough. He's got an away game in Cardiff tomorrow, so there's no point in me going down there this weekend, which is great news because I really don't like facing the cow when she's like this, she's just toxic.

*

Wednesday 29th November, 2000

I went for an interview today with a law firm in the City. There was a whole interview panel there, waiting to give me a grilling. Eight partners plus the head of HR, all men of course, with posh accents and dark suits. One guy asked me whether Bristol Public High School was really public, like he was making a joke but we all knew he was actually making a point.

I did that trick of imagining they were all in the nude, except instead of them being in the nude I tried to imagine they were all women, wearing dresses and high heels. How different that would feel.

Why did they even bother dragging me in to see them today? Probably to fulfil some bullshit equality quota they have.

*

Monday 11th December, 2000

Woohoo! Best news ever today!

Eighteen interviews with thirteen law firms across London over the last six weeks.

And...

I've been offered a training contract with Coulter & Co in Chancery Lane.

Starting in September 2002 after Law College.

I actually believe it now. I'm going to be a solicitor!

As soon as I get settled at Coulters I'll move Ryan in with me.

He'll be so excited when I tell him.

*

Tuesday 9th January, 2001

To do this week (and it's already Tuesday):

1. Jurisprudence essay
2. Prepare for moot
3. Finish first draft of dissertation
4. Employment Law essay
5. Prepare Employment Law seminar

This is everything that I should have got done over Christmas, but instead I was stacking shelves again.

Now I'm starting the term from behind and more work is coming in already.

And all because Mum would rather buy fags and booze than pay the rent.

*

Thursday 25th January, 2001

I was watching the cleaner dusting shelves in the library this morning, flicking her feather duster thingy around and humming happily to herself, and I realised I was envious of her. She's got no essays to write, no exams to pass, nothing to prove to herself or anyone else, a Pay packet at the end of the month. What else do you need?

I can only hope my future self will thank my current self for all this pain and suffering I'm putting myself through, that I'll think it was all worth it. Because at the moment, I'm thinking Mum was right all along and I should've stayed in Bristol and just led the life everyone thought I would.

*

Wednesday 14th February, 2001

I can't believe how sodding difficult this year is turning out to be.

My Employment Law essay failed so I have to re-do it by Friday. That's on top of everything else.

I feel physically sick with the pressure of it all. I can't even face making a list right now.

If I don't get through the next two weeks, I don't get to finish the year. No degree, no Law College, no Coulters.

I let myself down and I let Ryan down.

This is impossible. What the hell was I thinking???

25.

London

"Welcome to Britain, my beautiful girl," I tell Noura, planting a kiss on the top of her head as our cab joins the M4 motorway. I check the weather out of the window – 'dry and sunny' and 'a balmy eighteen degrees Celsius' as predicted by Captain Blankety Blank it certainly is not. The sky's dark and brooding, the low clouds heavy with unspent rain, and the occasional rumble in the distance confirms the brewing storm.

"Gonna rain again, innit?" says the cabbie, peering up at the sky and flicking on his headlights.

"Yes, shame," I say, but actually I love this weather: it's a welcome relief after the stifling heat and humidity we've left behind in Dubai. Noura, on the other hand, is looking terrified – like the bottom has fallen out of her world and she's landed in Hades instead of Heathrow. "Does the sun only live at home?" she says, rumpling her brows into a frown. I give her hand a squeeze. "Don't worry, the sun is still up there, sweetie. You just can't see it because it's hidden behind the clouds. It'll come out later once the storm has passed."

"Don't bank on it," chips in the cabbie. "I was supposed to be having a barbie with the missus and kids later, but that ain't gonna happen now by the looks of things. Bloody global warming, innit?"

That's a point, actually. At least when all this is behind us, I can revisit those subscriptions to Solar Cooking China and Wind Power Indonesia or whatever they're called. No more carbon footprint-induced guilt to offset – that's definitely a win. I glance at my watch: quarter past three. It's going to be tight but I don't have a choice – Tom was expecting my call at least half an hour ago. I ask the cabbie to stop at a phone shop on our way into London so I can pick up a new mobile and he takes us to a place on Harlington High Street. As soon as we're back on the road I call Tom and he picks up on the second ring.

"Yes, this is Tom Fletcher."

"Tom, it's me."

"Ah, thank God for that! Has everything gone to plan? You made it out okay with Noura?"

"I did, with some help from an unexpected source. Bloody Lubna got wind of us leaving and had her buddies escort us through the airport!"

"You're kidding?"

"Nope. I thought it was game over for a while but apparently Lubna had decided her life would be greatly improved without having to share it with Noura and me. She's got Amal all to herself now, hasn't she? What's the update with those two, anyway?"

"They're still on the loose, but not for much longer. I hear there's a synchronized dawn raid set up for tomorrow morning. Both homes and all sixteen stores. Amal and

Lubna have been tracked down to a hotel in Beirut so they'll be picked up there."

"Yes, right." I look over at Noura who's peering intently out the window up at the thunderous sky, her obsession with the Great British weather already begun.

"They're sharing the same room, by the way," Tom says.

"Ha, I knew it!" I'm trying to feel some vindication, but instead I just feel sad. Noura gives a little shiver and I squeeze her hand. "How about you, all okay?" I ask Tom.

"Yep. Everything's as expected this end. I activated roaming on your phone as soon as I landed in Delhi. There were a few missed calls and messages, as you'd expect," he chuckles. "Amal's asking where Noura is – the maid is frantic with worry and if you've taken her off for the day without asking again you'll have to deal with Fatima this time, blah, blah, blah. Alex says to remember to collect Josh from after-school football, four o'clock sharp. John Coulter got your resignation letter and wonders about you doing some *ad hoc* consultancy work for them instead. Mark wants you to call him back when you can. I think that's it."

"Thanks, Tom," I tell him. "You're nearly as good as Dimple at this secretarial malarkey."

"Sod off."

"Sod off yourself." I'm grinning as I disconnect.

The plan is that anyone looking for us will track my mobile to Delhi and the search will focus there first, buying us the extra time we need to disappear. We've planned out every step of the way, Tom and me, and the part of the plan we feared was most likely to fail – getting Noura out of Dubai – is done. *We're nearly there!* My stomach tingles every time I think about it. It's that feeling you get when you wake up on

AMBIGAMIST   189

the last day of exams, when you know a whole new, brighter
life is so, so close and a whole mass of horribleness is about
to be left behind. Coincidentally, I came across an article on
the plane earlier about 'decluttering your life'. Apparently
it's a thing now. The article was advocating a month-long
drive 'to help manage stress and boost your health by
banishing clutter and restoring a sense of order to your
world'. It struck me as apt and I gave myself the satisfying
task of making my 'chuck' and 'keep' lists resulting from
my own decluttering over the past month. *On my 'chuck' list:
Alex, Amal, James, Lubna, Fatima, my dark angel (finally),
housemaids in general, corporate sleaze, a double life, long-haul
commutes. And on my 'keep' list: Josh and Noura of course...*

"Nearly there," says the cabbie, slicing through my
private ramblings. "The traffic's been a complete 'mare this
afternoon, but we'll be there by four o'clock, don't worry."

In fact, it's quarter past four when we turn into the cul-
de-sac where Josh's school is. We're running late so he'll be
waiting out front, sat on the wall as usual. Except he isn't.
The school gates are locked, the cul-de-sac is deserted and
Josh is nowhere to be seen.

26.

London

I'm sat in the back of the cab and willing myself not to panic. *Breathe and think, just breathe and think. Where, where, where might he be?* Okay, maybe he's just taken himself home, simple as that. It's only a half hour walk from here and he knows the way.

"Take us to Chichester Row please, mate," I tell the cabbie.

"Right you are." He swings his cab around in a tight one-eighty turn and sets off back towards the high street. I'm scanning the pavements on both sides as we go. "Look for a blond boy dressed in a football kit," I tell Noura, "we can't go without him."

The mobile tracking app! I pull my iPad out of my bag and power it up. When Josh got his new phone the other day, I'd downloaded an app that lets me track all kinds of things on it – messages, calls, social networking activity, stored photos, and...GPS location. *Please, please, please let him have it with him today.* I open the app and it's asking for a password for Josh's account. *Oh god, what would I have used? Think, think.* I punch in Josh's date of birth in numerals followed by 'margo' in lowercase letters, but no joy. The taxi has stopped; we're at my house already. I grab my keys, dash out of the cab and shout back to Noura, "Just wait here baby, I'll be back in a jiffy!" as I charge up the steps to my front door. I let myself in and am greeted by calm and order. No Margo trotting up to say hello, because she's missing of course, no radio or television blaring, no feet stomping around, no breeze coming through from the open back door and, most tellingly, no school bags, shoes or other Josh-like paraphernalia in the hallway. I shout out my son's name, prepared for the silence that comes back at me. He's not here, but I refuse to believe he won't be found, to accept that my dark angel was right all along and I was never going to get to keep my children. I look at my watch and see that it's four thirty-five already. We're going to miss the boat. I dash back to the cab and grab my iPad. I punch in the password again, this time with a capital 'M' for Margo. *Thank God!* The app's responding. *Wait, wait. Yes!* A street map appears on the screen and right in the middle of it there's a beautifully pulsating blue circle. Josh's phone is apparently making its way down a street that's only three minutes away. I give the cabbie directions and off we go. Left, left, right, yes this is the street. There's a small person, down there, trotting along the pavement and looking in all the gardens. He's blond and wearing a football kit. Closer, closer. Yes, it's him.

"Josh! What on earth are you doing *here*?" I shout from the cab window as we get to him. "You're supposed to be waiting at the school." I sound angry, but I'm just relieved. "Thank God, we were so worried."

"I've been looking for Margo," he snaps at me, "because nobody else is." And then he bursts into tears. *God, I'm crap at this and I'm on my own now with these two,* I think. *What the hell am I doing?*

"Okay, okay, I get it," I say, holding up my hands in surrender. "But we need to get going, right now." I open the cab door and wave for him to get in. "C'mon, we're going on a journey."

"Really?" Josh swipes the tears off his cheeks and climbs into the cab.

"That's my boy." I take his bag and pull him into a hug. "Josh, this is Noura," I tell him, getting him seated. "We're going to be taking care of her from now on."

Josh takes his first look at his little sister and says, "Is she Margo's replacement?"

"No, of course not!" So much for that being a special moment to cherish. "We're still going to look for Margo, aren't we. Noura's extra."

"Then who is she? What's she doing here with us?"

"Do you remember I promised you by the time you're ten everything will have changed? Well, that change is starting today. We're going away to make a new life, and Noura's part of it."

"We're leaving without Margo?"

"You trust me, don't you?"

"Yes."

"Then let's go," I say, and ask the cabbie to take us to the train station by the quickest route he knows. Four forty-five. *Can we make the five o'clock train?* I sincerely hope so. If we miss it, we're buggered.

"I need your phone," I tell Josh once we're heading up the high street in the right direction.

"But..."

"Come on," I coax, holding out my hand. "We bought it so you could call me if ever you were in trouble, right? Well, now I'm right here with you so you don't need it anymore."

Josh sighs and hands over his phone and I get to the 'Erase iPhone' page without any difficulty. The taxi brakes and comes to a halt. I look out the window. We're stopped at red lights for a pedestrian crossing. The rain has started to lash down and is bouncing off the pavement. "Told you," the cabbie grumbles and the people out on the street scrabble to put up their umbrellas or huddle themselves tight and make a dash for it. The lights turn green and we move forward. I punch in the password, press return and, *Yes*, I've wiped the phone clean and it's back to factory settings. I remove the battery and SIM for good measure and kick all three pieces under the seat.

"Hey, there's Mr Green!" Josh raps his knuckles on the window to get the attention of one of the huddled-up people dashing down the street, and gives our next-door neighbour an enthusiastic wave when he looks our way. Mr Green, or 'Jim' as I know him, gives Josh an enthusiastic wave back and trots across to our practically stationary vehicle.

"You wouldn't be going home by any chance, would you?" Jim says when Josh puts down the window.

"No, sorry Mr Green, we're off on a..." Josh begins.

"...errand across town." I jump in, sitting forward in my seat to hide Noura from our neighbour's line of sight. "Sorry, we're in a bit of a rush."

"You're not going anywhere fast in this traffic," Jim says. There's rainwater dripping off the end of his nose. "Practically at a standstill, isn't it? Always the blooming same when it starts to rain. I was hoping you could give me a lift."

Now he's got his head through the window and is trying to peer behind me, looking at what ought to be an empty seat. Except it's not empty. I need to cut this off, right now. "Yep, anyway, good to see you Jim," I say, but as I jab at the button to put the window up I'm caught by a look of startled disgust from my son. Second thoughts. We'd be faster on foot anyway. "Just take it, it's all yours," I tell Jim, opening the cab door and pushing kids and bags out onto the pavement. "Here's a hundred towards the fare," I say, bundling some notes into his hand. I swing Noura up off her feet, grab the suitcase handle and start to leg it down the street. "C'mon Josh, we've got a train to catch."

By the time we reach Victoria train station we are a scary bunch to behold. Noura looks like a rag doll that's fallen into a lake, Josh is pebble-dashed with mud, remnants of football practice made sludgy with rain, and I'm wildly looking around for a ticket office, a departures board or a station master – anything or anyone that can help get us on that five o'clock train.

27.

London

Our train pulls out of Victoria station at five o'clock on the dot. Punctual to a tee, but there's a problem: we're not on it. It's leaving without us.

"Now what?" says Josh, as we stand on the platform watching the rear end of *Peter the Bloody Perfectly On-Time Engine* disappear from view. Good question. We could get a taxi, but in this rain, during rush hour? We'd never make it in time.

"We'll catch the next one," I say. That's a forty-minute wait, so I use the time to change the kids out of their wet clothes in the station loos and grab them some snacks from a kiosk. We're the first passengers to board the train because I'm taking no chances. Our luggage is stowed in the rack, we've taken seats where I can keep an eye on it and we're ready to go. Noura's tucking into a bag of Quavers, seeing how long she can get them to stick to her tongue, and Josh is staring out the window, mesmerized by the swarm of activity on the platform.

Right, there's no stopping us now. Next stop Southampton and then we're away, I think, relaxing back into the seat and closing my eyes. Alex will be getting home from the theatre just about now and expecting to see the veggies all chopped and diced ready for dinner and a nice Chablis cooling in the fridge. Wonder how long it will be before it occurs to that one to start making some calls? The penny will be slow to drop there, I suspect. Amal the crook will be out and about in downtown Beirut, arm-in-arm with the equally crooked Lubna, oblivious still to runaway families and dawn raids...

"Good evening ladies and gentleman..." The conductor's voice barges into my head and pops my eyes open. "Just to let you know, we're experiencing some delays in the departure of our trains this evening due to adverse weather conditions. We'll be on our way as soon as possible."

Adverse weather conditions? It's a bit of rain, for god's sake. The bloody five o'clock train managed to leave on time. I need to warn the guys at our rendezvous that we're running late. I pull out my phone and punch in the number I'd been given by the Somali businessmen the other day. Straight to voicemail. Damn! If our contacts are already outside coverage area, we're stuffed, but I'd told them we'd be there by seven o'clock, they're supposed to wait until at least then.

There's a clunk and a hiss and the train judders forward. Five fifty-five and we're on the move, gathering speed as we leave the station. I calculate our arrival time into Southampton Central and book an Uber on my iPad. I figure it's worth risking the web activity if it will get us there quicker. I rummage through my bag for the envelope I'd collected from the Somalis the other day and, finding it, I re-check its contents. Three new passports, three new birth certificates, all present and ready to back up our new identities when we reach our final destination: Kris, Joe and Norah Cote, Canadian by birth, South African by nationality. And I'm not a lawyer anymore, by the way, but a photographer, doing mainly portrait and corporate work, but also a wedding here and there because they pay really well. Plus there's my back portfolio of work that's never been published. And I could even do some freebie stuff for the nonprofits – that was important to me once, wasn't it? The possibilities are endless really. *Mmm, if I'd stuck with a career in photography in the first place I wouldn't be here, sat on this train...*

"We're there, we're there." I must have dozed off because Josh is shaking me awake and we're at Southampton Central already. At least one thing has gone our way today because the Uber's waiting for us when we exit the station. "Ocean Village please, mate," I tell the driver, "and delete my booking, if you don't mind. My credit card's maxed so I'll pay in cash."

"No worries," he says, "suits me fine."

By the time we reach the marina, the sun's poking through the few remaining clouds, promising one of those glorious raspberry ripple sunsets. And guess what? We'll get to see it from the water. We find the right jetty and walk down it, looking for our next transportation, a thirty-five metre motor yacht going by the name of *African Duchess* and selected for the job by my new Somali friends. Here it is, berth eight. Except the berth's empty. We've missed the bloody boat.

"You alright over there?"

The voice is coming from a wooden fishing vessel three berths down. *Oh my god, it's Captain Birdseye,* is my first thought, because he's got the blue peaked cap, the white facial hair, the brass-buttoned blazer, all of it going on. *He could be our knight in shining armour*, is my second thought.

"You haven't seen a boat called *African Duchess* around here, by any chance?" I venture. "We're supposed to be joining them on board."

"Left half hour ago."

"Oh bugger. I've been trying to call them but they must be out of range already. You're not heading that way, are you?"

"What? Out to sea? No, afraid not. I'm done for the day."

"Is there any chance at all you could take us out to the *African Duchess*? We really do need to get on that boat."

"That's quite a favour you're asking there," he says. He looks up at the sky and down at his watch and scratches his beard. "Wife's away, though," he continues, "so I guess I could." Then he starts to look us up and down a little more closely. "You're not trafficking kids or anything like that, are you?" he asks.

"Haha! No, nothing like *that*," I say, with the innocent air of the guilty. "They're both mine, I can assure you," I quickly add. Josh is nodding vigorously and Noura's smiling sweetly at Captain Birdseye whilst I'm delving into my bag. "Here's our passports if you'd like to check."

"Nah, you're okay," he says. "Let's get you all aboard, then."

28.

Saturday 18th March, 2001

The Marshalls confirmed today. That's 5 photography jobs lined up for the Easter hols. Six if the theatre job comes through.

Spoke to Ryan this morning and he wants me to come home for Easter. I explained I can't now I've got this photography work to do but I promised to get him the new Chelsea football shirt instead.

If I can afford it, I'll get him the shorts and socks too.

He's a great kid and deserves so much more than Mum gives him. I don't mean only material things, but care, love, praise, encouragement, all those other things parents are supposed to provide.

He'll get all of that by the lorryload when he comes to live with me next September.

*

Sunday 15th April, 2001

Easter Sunday!

I surprised Mum and Ryan and got the train down to Bristol for the day.

Mum was in bed, so nothing new there. She claimed to have flu, but it seems to be of the permanent kind if that's true. I had a great time with Ryan though. He loved the football kit I brought him. I took him and his mate Oliver to see *Spy Kids* at the cinema and we went for pizza afterwards.

Ryan surprised me by asking about Dad. He was just a baby when he left, so he doesn't have any memories of him. He was hoping we could find Dad and he could go and live with him until I was ready to have him. I told him to forget it, both our parents are a dead loss and we're better off taking care of ourselves.

Roll on September 2002.

*

Thursday 24th May, 2001

The finishing line is in sight. Final exams start on Monday and I can't wait to get them over with.

I've got some major cramming to do over the next couple of weeks. I'd like to have fitted in a trip down to Bristol to see Ryan, make sure he's doing okay, but I really can't.

I'll see him when I've finished. It's just two weeks away.

*

Monday 28th May, 2001

Ryan called today, but I was in the middle of a test paper so Richard had a chat with him instead. He'd phoned to wish me luck with the exams, which was really thoughtful for an eleven-year-old. I'll call him back tomorrow to say thanks and to see how he's doing.

*

Thursday 31st May, 2001

Exams are going okay so far. No major disasters that I'm aware of. A question on health and safety came up in the employment exam today, which was annoying because I hadn't revised that properly, but I've hopefully done enough to pass anyway.

I've just remembered I was supposed to call Ryan back, but it's eleven o'clock at night now so he'll be sleeping. I'll call tomorrow.

*

Tuesday 5th June, 2001

It's my last exam tomorrow and I am so excited. I'm not going to get a wink of sleep tonight, but that's okay, the excitement will be enough to get me through to tomorrow evening. So close, but not quite there yet. I bet it will be a real anti-climax, though!

I've decided that after my exam tomorrow, I'm going to get myself down to Bristol to meet Ryan from school. Since he's always been there every step of the way, spurring me on, we should celebrate the end of Uni together. I'll take him to the amusement park, he loves the roller-coaster and dodgems there. It'll make up for me not calling him in ages. I'll still be able to get back here in time for our house party tomorrow night.

*

Wednesday 6th June, 2001

The phone in the hall was ringing when I got back from my last exam this morning.

It was Mum. Bloody hell, I thought, that's a first, she must be calling to congratulate me.

How wrong I was.

She was calling to tell me Ryan died last night.

29.

Southampton

"I'll just get us out of the marina and then you can take the wheel," Captain Birdseye, *aka* Jasper Pullins, tells me.

"Are you sure? I've never steered one of these before," I say.

"Well, you either take the helm or operate the radio, whichever you prefer."

The kids are sat in the cockpit at this point, immobilised by the adult-sized life jackets Jasper insisted they put on. Josh has already told Noura she looks like SpongeBob SquarePants, which they found hilarious, of course, and had the two of them in fits of giggles, but they've settled down now and they're both looking at me with lingering amusement.

"I'll take the helm, then," I say, shooting them a warning look.

"Right you are," says my new pal Jasper, who's reversing us out of the berth and getting us pointed towards the sea. "We'll get ourselves into clear water first, then I'll try putting a call out over the radio to see if the *African Duchess* responds."

Of course, there's radio! Oh god, let's hope that works.

"Yes, that will work," I say confidently, because the kids are watching, still happy, still amused by events, their trust in me still intact.

But what's the plan if we don't catch up with the African Duchess?

"Over to you, then," Jasper says, releasing one arm from the wheel and waving me forwards. "Just keep us going straight ahead, gentle movements that's all that's needed, there's nothing to it really."

Jasper goes down a couple of steps and disappears into the cabin, leaving me and the kids above deck. There are quite a few other boats out on the water, I notice, mostly small sailing yachts helping their owners to blow away cobwebs after their day at work. I can't see anything that looks remotely like an *African Duchess*, what I know to be a thirty-five metre motor yacht. I pull out my phone and try calling her crew again, just in case, but it goes straight to voicemail and I leave yet another message, again, just in case.

I shake my head as I rewind the clock, re-examining the decisions that have brought us all here today, right here and now in the English Channel, aboard this rickety wooden fishing boat owned by a complete stranger and chasing after a motor yacht crewed by a bunch of Somali 'fishermen'.

Well, there was no new Coulters office to open in Dubai and the job offer from Shamal Enterprises was a complete non-starter, so I'd had to choose between London or Dubai or the highway – those were the options. And then there was Josh and Noura to consider, the most important people in the equation. Should I have stayed in London, settled back into Coulters full-time, and left Noura to be brought up by a maid and an eccentric grandmother, both her parents absent? No thanks! Even if Amal wasn't headed for prison, it's not the upbringing I want for my daughter. But if I'd brought her to live in London, we'd have been swiftly tracked down from Dubai and torn apart. Should I have got myself a permanent position in Dubai, then, settled down there and left Josh in the hands of a drunken, neglectful parent? Been there, done that, and it had resulted in my brother's death. But neither could I have taken Josh with me to live in Dubai – we would have been tracked down from London in five minutes. Bad Cop would have had a field day with that one, wouldn't she?

So 'the highway' it was.

My logic is no doubt warped from the harsh lessons of Ryan's death but, nonetheless, how could I have solved all of this differently?

"Okay, so the *African Duchess* has responded to the call." Jasper has re-emerged from below deck and he's on a mission, all fired up. "They want to know who we are," he puffs. "They say they can't turn around for a boat called *Lunasea*."

Josh sniggers, which sets Noura off, and there they go again in a fit of giggles like it's the funniest thing they've ever heard.

"Tell them *Ryan's legacy*," I say to Jasper, trying to ignore them. "It's a password. They'll know."

"Right you are," he replies, but just as he's about to go and continue his conversation with the *African Duchess* the smooth hum of the engine starts to break up and sputter, so instead he comes over and fiddles with a couple of the controls next to the wheel. "Bloody thing's been running rough on and off all day," he grumbles, bringing the engine back to a smooth hum and disappearing down into the cabin.

But he hasn't been gone long before there's a *putt, putt, putt* from the engine, followed by a loud *bang* from under our feet and tendrils of smoke and the smell of burning permeate the slats of the wooden deck. *Crap, we're on fire!* I think, but it all quickly dissipates, and now there's only silence. The kids are looking at me if to say 'so what now?' but there's still no fear, no flicker of doubt on their faces.

"Right," says Jasper, making an appearance from below deck. "The engine's buggered, that's the bad news."

"And the good news?" I say.

"The *African Duchess* says it's turning around and coming back to collect you all. We'll put down anchor here and wait for them."

"That's brilliant!" I say. "I don't know how to thank you enough, helping us out like this, and I'm so sorry to have caused you all this trouble."

"Don't think anything of it, it's the most excitement I've had in years," Jasper says, making his way up to the prow. He drops the anchor overboard and feeds the rope through his roughened hands before pulling back to check the anchor has caught on the seabed. "So, *Ryan's legacy*, what's that all about?" he says, making his way back to the cockpit.

"Ryan was my brother," I say, "and this trip we're on is all about respecting his legacy. Nothing more than that, really."

"Well, good luck," he says, clearly getting the hint. "I hope it all turns out well for you."

"Thanks, me too."

The boat's beginning to rock a bit now we're anchored, I notice, and the breeze is building as the sun's dropping behind the clouds.

"Getting a bit squally," Jasper says, looking up at the sky. "But the *African Duchess* will be here soon, so there's nothing to worry about. So, kids," he says, turning his attention to Josh and Noura, "do you two always get on well, then, or do you argue sometimes like most brothers and sisters?"

"It's too early to say really," Josh replies.

"Pardon?"

Jasper's looking confused by this response so Josh quickly says, "We only met each other this afternoon."

Oh Lord!

"I think I can hear the radio," I say. "Maybe it's the *African Duchess* trying to get hold of us?"

"Bloody hearing," says Jasper, sticking his finger in his ear and jiggling it around. "It's getting worse by the day, I'm afraid," he says, making his way down into the cabin.

"This is *Lunasea*," we then hear from below decks and I shoot Josh a stern look of warning. He clamps his lips together tightly and looks up to the sky.

"Please repeat your last message, we didn't quite catch it."

A sudden clap of thunder drowns out the reply and the first drops of rain spot the wooden deck.

"I suggest you get yourselves down here out of the rain," says Jasper, poking his head out from the cabin.

"I want to stay up here," says Noura, "I haven't seen rain before."

"Don't be silly Noura," I say, "of course you have."

"Not really," she insists. "I've never been out in it before, anyway."

"So where have you been living all your life?" Jasper asks her jokingly. "In the desert?"

"Take no notice, she's always making stuff up," I say, jumping in quickly. "It's the age, isn't it?"

"It certainly is! My granddaughter's just the same, living in a world of her own, all fairy tales and whatnot. Talking of which," Jasper says, looking out over the water, "here's our very own Sir Galahad coming to the rescue now." He's pointing at a white boat that's heading rapidly towards us. There's at least three men on board, two up on the bridge and one on the prow, and they're all waving at us in a friendly enough fashion as far as I can make out.

"Hello there," says Jasper as they draw alongside us. "Any chance of getting a tow back to shore?"

30.

English Channel

So apparently, the crew of the *African Duchess* had thought they were still on Central European Time and set sail an hour early. In their minds, the kids and I weren't going to make the rendezvous so they'd gone into emergency getaway mode, ditching any incriminating evidence, turning off phones and making a hasty departure up the Solent. Anyway, we're all safely aboard now and I need to call Mark before my mobile loses signal.

"Mark! It's Chris, calling from the English Channel."

"Ah, you're away okay then? We're missing you already, just so you know."

"Glad to hear it. Everything alright there? Did it all go to plan?"

"Yep, plain sailing, hahah. As you instructed, I 'found' the lost due diligence documents 'whilst clearing out my office desk' last night. Dimple was only too happy to come back in to work this morning and upload them to the data room. But not before I'd had that little chat with Al Shamsi. The prospect of being banged up in a Dubai jail serving time for blackmail, bribery and conspiracy to defraud for the next umpteen years, not to mention the disgrace it would bring upon his family's name in the local Emirati community, was more than enough to convince him to pay the full amount without any fuss. So, Bailey's Dubai is now sold, bang on fifty million dollars."

"That's great news, Mark, I'm really pleased for you. You've exited Dubai with a tidy profit and now you can get on with that casino project."

"Ah, yes, about that. Grace has dug her heels in and put a stop to that one."

"Has she?" I reply innocently.

"Yes, she says we're both due a break so I've had to flick it on. Did okay on it, though."

"Of course, I wouldn't expect anything less," I say, grinning. *Thank you, Grace, you've saved your husband from getting himself into a nasty legal quagmire there.*

"I got a little bonus thrown in, by the way. You know that photo you got of Al Shamsi canoodling with his floozie in the back of a London cab?"

"Yes, it's a cracker."

"Well, I agreed we wouldn't make it public in return for him agreeing to change the name of the company – so I don't have to let them use my name after all. *Bailey's Dubai* has now officially been renamed *Shamal Sands*," Mark says with a chuckle. "Al Shamsi and Haddad also know to stay shtum about you, by the way. I've told them both I'm keeping the voice recordings and all the other evidence we've got against them as insurance for their continued silence."

"That's great. Thanks, Mark." At least they won't be spilling the beans to Amal or Alex any time soon and helping them piece things together.

Amal will be contacting the authorities in Delhi and desperately urging them to search for Noura and me there, whilst

*back in England Alex will be feverishly phoning around all
our friends and family to see if Josh and I are with them before
reaching the grim conclusion that this is a case for the police.
Eventually the two separate investigations will collide and then
run dry, and my spouses will jointly mourn the fact that we've
disappeared from their lives forever...*

Hah! Who am I tying to kid?

The much more likely scenario would go something
like this:

GOOD COP: Thanks for joining us on this video call today.
We wanted to update you on our search for Chris and
the kids. Well, really, to tell you both that unfortunately
we've run out of leads at this point.

BAD COP: Not that either of you have been much help
along the way, have you?

AMAL: What do you expect? I've been banged up in here
all month.

ALEX: Oh dear, darlings, I've been as helpful as I can but
I'm not terribly good at this sort of thing.

BAD COP: Is that champagne you're drinking?

ALEX: Good lord, no! This is just some cheap bubbly
stuff I picked up at the supermarket. I ran out of
champagne weeks ago after Chris deserted me. It's all
been *very* distressing, I have to tell you!

See! Mark was right! Your bloody booze mule, that's all I was to you in the end.

GOOD COP: Oh yes, very distressing I'm sure. Awful! Just awful!

BAD COP: So, moving along, subject to anything further either of you has to say, we are now going to be closing the case.

AMAL: Fine by me, go ahead and close it. To be honest, the prison I'm in now is better than the one Chris had me living in for the last three years, nagging me to play happy families all the time. Yuck!

No, Amal, I just wanted you to spend some quality time with Noura. And I never wanted to marry you in the first place – you were just a fling.

BAD COP: What are you banged up for, anyway? Heard it was money laundering. Has your runaway Chris got anything to do with it, by any chance?

AMAL: Our perfect little Chris? Are you kidding?

BAD COP: Not so perfect, actually. There is the small issue of the bigamy...

GOOD COP: Alex, are you still with us?

[silence]

[Bad Cop slams fist loudly on table]

ALEX: Eh? What? Yes, I'm still here.

GOOD COP: Okay, good. It looked like you may have nodded off there for a moment.

They look at Alex and see a lush, don't they? How sad. Where did it go to, Alex, all that ambition and promise that once defined you?

BAD COP: We were saying, we're going to close the case...

ALEX: Oh, yes, please do! Don't keep it open on my account, darlings.

GOOD COP: Terrific! We'll consider the case closed, then. But just before we let you go, I'm curious, why do you think Chris decided to take the kids? Wouldn't it have been easier to just disappear and leave the kids behind with you guys?

[Horrified expressions from Amal and Alex]

BAD COP: Are you kidding? Just look at them both!

Maybe things will be different one day – Amal might grow up whilst in prison, and Alex might sober up with some professional help. I hope so. When the time is right I'll make room for them both to come back into our lives. But for now, it's just the three of us, on a boat heading south, safe in the hands of five Somali pirates.

EPILOGUE

Several weeks later

I was never sure what our exact date of arrival in Cape Town would be: that was always dependent on the weather conditions at sea and us being able to make our connections from one vessel to another as we made our way down the west coasts of Europe and Africa. But here we are, the three of us back on terra firma. We've got new passports, new birth certificates, new identities. This is the start of our new life in a new country.

I haven't spoken with the outside world since my call to Mark all those weeks ago as we were sailing from Southampton, so I'm feeling quite nervous as we pile out of a taxi, stride up a garden path and knock on a door. There's someone at home because we can hear footsteps. They're pounding towards the front door as loudly as my heart is pounding in my chest. Both children are looking up at me anxiously and I give them a reassuring smile. The door's thrown open to reveal a man and a dog.

"Tom!" My voice is a strangled yelp as I'm pulled into a tight hug. Tom Fletcher. Managing partner of Hattan & Co's new Cape Town office, and also my second (or is it third?) chance at getting things right.

Josh is studying the dog intently. The dog is sniffing Josh. Their moment of mutual recognition is like one of those soppy videos that go viral on Facebook: the dog lets out a yelp and starts to skip around, wagging its tail furiously as Josh bursts into tears and drops to his knees. "Margo!" Josh squeals, hugging the friend he thought he'd lost. "How did you get here?"

Noura, meanwhile, is looking unusually serious. "That's not Margo," she says, "that's Charlie."

ACKNOWLEDGEMENTS

Huge thanks to my editor, Laurie Gibson, not only for her superb editing skills, but also for her encouragement and friendship at a pivotal time. Likewise, my thanks to Tony Bonds, my book designer, bonus beta reader and all-round troubleshooter.

Thank you to my early beta readers for their courage to pick up the manuscript and their patience in offering invaluable feedback – Giles Dale, Gary Scott, Tracey Still, Steve Bainbridge, Kimberley Foulkes and Lisa Evans. You have no idea how much you helped with getting this book out of the drawer and into the world!

Annabel Kantaria and Jessica Jarlvi, book club friends and published authors, thank you for being amazing trailblazers.

Stephen McGowan, thank you for your advice on casino licensing regulations: I owe you a scotch!

Thanks to the corporate world of Dubai for providing a ton of inspiration; beautiful Cyprus, for being the perfect place to write; and the writing community of San Diego, for getting *Ambigamist* to publication.

Finally, we'd be nowhere without family. Thank you to my parents, for being the source of my determination; George and Chloe, for cheering me on; and Giles, for many things. I love you all!

ABOUT THE AUTHOR

Lisa Dale is an English Solicitor. After qualifying in 1993, she spent seven years practising law in Great Britain before moving to Dubai with her family in 2000. There, she was a partner with a local law firm before retiring from the law in 2016. She is currently living in San Diego, California with her husband. *Ambigamist* is her first novel.

Lightning Source UK Ltd.
Milton Keynes UK
UKHW041538140620
364912UK00005B/1382